W9-CTT-075

Sydney moved stealthily through the dark room, intent on getting to the kids and getting them out of there fast.

Seconds before she was jumped, she spun around, her hands raised to deflect an attack. Her first blow met a bare, rock-hard stomach.

The man's muttered curse told her she'd achieved her goal. But she fought on, until she had him pinned to the floor. Straddling his body, she realized his bottom half was as bare as his top half.

"Auntie Syd!" Heidi piped. "That man isn't wearing any clothes!"

"Jamie, take your sister into the kitchen," Sydney shouted, although her warning was a little late. "I'll get up nice and easy, and so will you," she said in a level voice, once the kids were gone. "I can take you down anytime, so don't try anything."

"No problem." Ki reached for a blanket to wrap around his waist, pleased to notice her covert glance downward.

"What are you doing here?" she demanded.

"I *own* one-fourth of this place. What's your excuse?"

Dear Reader,

You're about to step under the mistletoe with one of our four hunky heroes this month in our CHRISTMAS KISSES holiday promotion!

For Linda Randall Wisdom, December is a special month. Fifteen years ago this month she got a combination Christmas/anniversary present with the sale of her first two books. A year later, in December, her first book was published.

Linda and all of us at Harlequin wish you a joyous holiday filled with CHRISTMAS KISSES!

Merry Christmas!

Debra Matteucci
Senior Editor and Editoral Coordinator
Harlequin Books
300 E. 42nd Street
New York, NY 10017

Linda Randall Wisdom

HE'S A REBEL

Harlequin Books

TORONTO • NEW YORK • LONDON
AMSTERDAM • PARIS • SYDNEY • HAMBURG
STOCKHOLM • ATHENS • TOKYO • MILAN
MADRID • WARSAW • BUDAPEST • AUCKLAND

ISBN 0-373-16561-7

HE'S A REBEL

Prologue

"You're not listening to me, Leo. I'm quitting. I'm getting out of the business."

"This is a joke, right? You're trying to give me an ulcer by claiming you're getting out. No tricks, Sydney. Just tell me when you're coming back to D.C., which better be within the next twenty-four hours. I need you for an upcoming assignment. It's right up your alley. No one can handle this the way you can. Listen to me, babe. This is too important for you to take off and play Mommy."

Sydney Taylor looked out the phone booth's dingy Plexiglas siding toward the black Jeep Cherokee she had parked nearby. As far as she was concerned, the only things important in her life were the two small faces plastered against the windows. They watched her with anxious expressions as if they feared she would suddenly disappear from their sight. She pictured her superior, sitting behind his desk dressed in a rumpled gray suit and chewing on a cigar. She once told him he always sounded like one of those sleazy theatrical agents you'd see in a thirties movie.

"I'm not coming back, Leo. To D.C. or to the agency. I know you don't like people quitting, but when have I ever done what you expected me to?"

"*Never!* Syd, you're killing me here!" Leo Birch, director of a government agency that handled international crimes, screamed through the telephone. "Nobody quits us and you know it." His voice suddenly turned cajoling. "What are you looking for? Perks? No problem. Whatever you want, sweetheart. We're here for you, you know that."

Syd shook her head. Leo's idea of keeping his people happy was to use bribery in the worst way. He'd flush out their weaknesses and use them to his advantage. It was a well-known fact among the agents. The best-known story was Chaz Roberts spending a hot weekend with the actress of his dreams. Sydney tried to remember if she'd ever made jokes about seducing a particular man.

"We can do this real easy." He took a deep breath. "You can have your own Sweet Treat franchise."

Syd groaned. He'd headed straight for her weak spot. The Sweet Treat candy shops carried her absolute favorite candy and everyone knew it. If anyone wanted a little help they'd just mention a box of the candy and she was theirs.

"Great try, Leo. I really appreciate the thought, but no thanks. I've got two kids to look after now." She thought of her niece and nephew who needed her more than the agency did.

"You think I don't have a heart? You think I don't have feelings? This may be hard for you to believe, but there's blood running through these veins, Syd. The veins I'll probably have to open because you're killing me here. You won't have to worry about those kids while you're in Marseilles. I'll have my secretary find the best boarding school in the area. Hell, we'll even pick up the tab. You won't have to worry about a thing while you're gone. They'll be well taken care of," her boss assured her.

"Leo, they don't need a boarding school, they need security," she told him. "They lost both parents in one fell swoop. All they have is me, and I intend to make sure they don't lose *me* because I've gone out and don't come back. They need to know there's always someone there for them. Don't worry, I'll send you my resignation in writing, so everything will be official. You won't have any problem replacing me."

"Won't have any problem? Damn right, I won't! But I don't want to go to the trouble of training someone else and I don't want your damn resignation! I want you back here, so I can send you on your next assignment!"

"No."

"Come on, Syd. I'd make a better mother than you would. Sorry, honey, it's just not in your mental makeup."

Syd tried to visualize the balding Leo singing a lullaby while chomping on one of his favorite cigars. It didn't work.

"You forget, Leo. I have an edge. I can stand being around children. Don't talk to me about whether I can do this or not. If I can disarm a bomb without breaking a nail, I can handle two kids."

Syd held the receiver away from her ear as her ex-boss screamed every threat known to man and a few new ones even she hadn't heard of.

"Very inventive, Leo. I swear, no one can come up with threats the way you can. All I can say is get over it. I'm outta there."

"You can't stay away and you know it. You need the danger and excitement. You feed on it the same way a vampire feeds on blood."

Sydney grimaced at his comparison. "Thanks, Leo, that really makes me more convinced I need to get out while I still can. Look at it this way. You always accused me of never doing what you want me to do and now I'm proving you right."

"We'll find you!"

"I doubt it. You may be good, but you always said I was better." Without a hint of guilt, Syd hung up.

She offered a reassuring smile to the children as she walked back to her Jeep. She opened the door and looked at the little girl and boy ensconced in the back seat along with two dogs leaping from back seat to front.

"Are we going home, Aunt Syd?" the little girl asked with a solemn, wide-eyed gaze.

She reached across the seat and brushed the child's bangs away from her eyes. "No, Heidi, not right now, but I promise we'll go somewhere very nice."

"Are we running away? Daddy always said your boss wouldn't let you quit," the boy told her. "If he won't let you quit, you'll have to go away."

"No, I won't be going away," she stated emphatically.

"What are we going to do, Auntie Syd?"

Syd's heart clenched as she thought of her brother. Shane, her twin brother who hadn't deserved to die. Shane, her peace-loving brother who protested when a mugger wanted his wife's purse and lost his life as a result. She thought of Jenny, also dying because she fought back when confronted with the sight of her husband's bleeding body. And she thought of Syd, the woman who vowed never to marry. Syd, who told her brother it was a good thing he wanted kids, because she doubted she'd be a good mother, and who was now in charge of two childrens' lives.

Syd, who never flinched when facing a gun or a knife, and who was now scared to death as she realized her future had made a 360-degree turn.

She patted the honey-blond curly wig that concealed her copper-penny hair and shifted in the tight jeans and sweater that revealed the curves she normally didn't advertise. With the heavy makeup covering her face, she looked as if she belonged on a street corner cooing, "Hey sailor, new in town?"

"We're going to take a vacation, Jamie," she assured her nephew as she started up the engine. "Believe me, we're going to have a lot of fun."

Chapter One

"I can't believe my eyes! Ki, wha'cha doin' out this way at this time of year?" Jedidiah, owner of Jedidiah's Stop & Shop, greeted the man who walked into the small store.

Ki Jones's craggy face broke into a smile. "Hi Jedidiah. How are you doing?"

"The tourists keep me busy." He watched Ki wander through his general store filling a blue plastic shopping basket with the necessities of life, among them beer, Doritos, pretzels and cheese. "Ain'cha gonna pick up something other than junk food? My Sarah would have my hide if she knew I was lettin' you pick up food guaranteed not to fill your belly."

"We always leave plenty of staples up at the cabin, so I'm sure there's more than enough up there to keep me from starving." Ukiah, aka Ki, juggled a few candy bars in time to the Barking Dogs doing their rendition of "Jingle Bells" over the store's loudspeaker. "I figured I'd pick up a few extras before I got up there. Anything been happening around here other than the tourists?"

The older man shook his head. "Not near as exciting as when you boys are up here. You four always gave us old-timers somethin' to talk about!"

Ki smiled. Only Jedidiah would consider him and his three friends boys, when they were all pretty well past the thirty mark.

"We believe in doing our best," he said modestly. "Say, is Zeke still around?"

"Sure is. Knowing Zeke, he'll probably outlast us all just 'cause he's so ornery." Jedidiah shook his head in amazement. "Word is he built another still right after the sheriff dismantled his old one. Sheriff went up there snooping a couple weeks ago, but he couldn't find anything. He told Zeke he better not hear of him selling the stuff or he'll spend the rest of his days in jail. You know Zeke, he told the sheriff to put his advice where the sun don't shine."

Ki thought of the liquor Zeke, an old hermit who lived nearby, brewed. He and the others used to say only a tiny sip burned holes in your stomach! "The sheriff ought to give up looking. Zeke's smarter'n all of us put together. I heard the only reason the other still was found was because a fisherman got lost and stumbled onto it."

"That's true. I'm surprised you're back up here since it hasn't been all that long since the weddin'."

"It seemed like a good idea." Ki reached for a box over his head, then winced as sore muscles protested. He had no idea his buddy could grab him and throw him against the wall so easily. Oh, well, if he hadn't been so plastered he would have thought about ducking. The idea he shouldn't have made the remark about Tripp's wife-to-be in the first place didn't even occur to him. After all, the nickname he'd used was what they had called her back at Beckett!

"Can't believe you're all gettin' married." Jedidiah looked stunned. "Hell, I never thought it would happen. We thought you would all stay bachelors like you all vowed to do. Boy, you're not thinkin' of gettin' married, too, are ya?"

Ki burst out laughing. "Me? What woman in her right mind would have me?"

"There's the catch. She wouldn't be in her right mind!" Jedidiah cackled, slapping his knee in delight.

He grinned. "Yeah, well, I'm still doing things in my own way. Steve and Tripp might like being shackled to one woman, but I'm happier knowing I can pick up and take off whenever I want without having to explain why."

Jedidiah nodded. "I hear ya. Say, you're not going to stay up at the cabin for Christmas, are you? I'd think you'd be going out to see your mom."

He shook his head. "I've got a deadline snapping at me, and I need some peace and quiet to finish my book. I figured the best place to do that was the cabin. What made it easier for me was my mom and her husband decided to take their belated honeymoon now." Privately, Ki's idea of celebrating the holidays was to take off for a warm climate and generally take an even warmer woman with him.

"Who're you writing about now? I remember that last book about that man who killed all those people in that small town. It was downright scary. You seemed to get right into his nasty little mind. How he got away with all those murders for so long was amazing. Whose mind are you gettin' into this time?"

Ki paused a beat before answering. "Thomas Baskin."

"Woowee, that's one bad man." Jedidiah shook his head in amazement. "I read all about him. The newspapers said he'd get married, then kill his wives. Did you talk to him?"

Ki nodded. "Yeah, I just spent the last three months in Chicago interviewing him. Believe me, he's as bad in person as the media made him out to be. Trouble is, he comes across so charming that it takes you a minute to remember that it was his charm that killed a lot of women." He turned his head and looked out the window toward the parking lot as he heard the heavy thump of a truck door close.

His attention immediately zeroed in on the new customer. "Will you look at that. I'd say your class of clientele is looking up."

The older man's eyes almost bugged out as he watched a curvy blond-haired woman gingerly walk up the concrete walkway toward the glass doors. Dressed in electric blue spandex pants, matching suede half boots and a fuchsia fake-fur waist-length jacket, she would have caught any man's eye. But it was the body encased in the figure-hugging clothing that caught Ki's eye. Talk about a compact package of femininity! She was more than enough to make a man stand at attention.

"Something tells me she should have turned left instead of right at the crossroads," Ki said wryly, unable to keep his eyes off the length of leg. "She looks as if she's heading for a night at the casinos instead of a ski lodge."

A quick blast of icy air hit the two men as the woman pushed the glass door open and stepped inside.

"Excuse me, gentlemen," she said in a syrupy southern drawl. "But ah was wonderin' if y'all could tell me how to get back to the main highway? I seem to have lost my way."

Jedidiah puffed up. "Why, I sure can, miss." He walked over and immediately rambled off a set of directions. Ki hung back and pretended to study the back of a box of crackers while he surreptitiously studied the woman.

He always liked his women petite and fluffy, and this woman was not close to being considered petite. He figured she had to stand a good five ten in bare feet. She had a lean body that looked more like it belonged to a professional athlete than a party girl, tousled, honey-blond, shoulder-length curls that would do Dolly Parton proud and enough makeup on her face to cover five women.

He'd guess she wasn't all that much younger than his thirty-three years, although thanks to modern science it was getting more difficult to tell a woman's age. That was when he noticed her eyes. She tried to project a guileless nature, but her eyes gave her away. They were too sharp and watchful. They didn't fit the picture of the party girl she was conveying, but he doubted most people, especially men, would notice her eyes—except the incredible color—when they could look at her body instead. He would hazard a guess that she had catalogued everything, and everyone, in the store within five seconds of walking inside. They weren't the eyes of a fluff-brain.

He wondered why she felt she had to put on an act. Then the most logical thought came to mind. She could be on the run. If anyone knew about a person with a predator's skill, it was him. He'd met more than his share over the years as he traveled the country meeting with and interviewing major criminals as subjects for the increasingly popular true-crime books he wrote.

As if sensing his thoughts on her, the woman turned her head and looked over her shoulder at him.

No woman has eyes that intense shade of blue, he thought, feeling them probe him from head to toe. He felt as if she knew everything about him from his shoe size up to the tiny scar in his scalp from a badly thrown pitch during junior varsity baseball in high school.

"Is there a problem, sir?" she asked in that drawl that threatened to suffocate him in tons of cotton.

"Not a one, sweetheart. Not a one. Just enjoying the view." He flashed his trademark grin. The one that had seduced more than one woman into falling into his arms—and his bed. He held his hands up in surrender as if he was about as dangerous as a tiny kitten.

Not by a flicker of an eyelash did she indicate that she found his rugged good looks fascinating or that his grin sent waves of heat through her body. She turned around as if he wasn't worth the effort. She picked up several packs of gum and breath mints and pulled a couple of bills out of her jacket pocket. "Who could

I talk to about finding a place around here to rent or lease?" She spoke to Jedidiah.

The older man replied. "This time of year, places are usually already taken. A lot of people like to come up for skiing during the holidays. But you can check at the real estate office to see if there's anything available." He then went on to give more directions.

Ki took his time loading up on supplies. He added coffee and eggs to the pile of groceries while covertly watching her. He glanced outside and noticed the black Jeep Cherokee parked next to his truck. He frowned as he thought he saw movement inside.

"Thank you so much." The woman's sultry voice sounded suddenly loud to him, drawing his attention from the parking lot. She didn't look at Ki as she walked back outside and climbed into the Jeep.

Jedidiah stood behind the counter, rubbing his chin as he stared through the glass. "Now, that's what I'd call a red-blooded woman."

"Good thing Sarah's not around to hear you say that," Ki teased, setting the basket on the counter. "She'd have you sleeping on the living room couch for the next ten years."

"Come on, Ki. You can't tell me you wouldn't want her for a neighbor. I know you boys usually go up to your place to get away from women, but you're on your own this time. Once the women in Tahoe find out, they're going to be pounding on your door. You might as well take advantage of it."

Ki shook his head. "Hard as it is to believe, Jedidiah, women are the last thing on my mind this trip. I intend to get this book done on time." He looked outside. "Looks as if we're going to have another snowfall soon. Guess I'd better get up to the cabin before it gets too dark."

Jedidiah loaded everything into plastic shopping bags and rang up the total. "You got the utilities turned on?"

Ki nodded. "I made the calls just before I left Chicago." He picked up the bags. "See ya, Jedidiah."

When Ki walked outside, he looked up at the gray sky and calculated he had enough time to get up to the cabin before more snow started falling. His boots made crunching sounds on the hard-packed snow as he crossed the parking lot to his four-wheel-drive vehicle and placed the bags in the back. He looked at the tracks the Jeep had left behind. The woman might have looked like a ditz, but the tire tracks told him they were obviously used for hard driving. He climbed behind the wheel and started up the engine. As he waited for the heater to kick in, he thought about the blonde.

"Why would a woman who looked as if she belonged in some fancy, low-slung foreign car be all the way out here driving a Jeep?" he mused, putting the truck in gear.

"AUNTIE SYD, I HAVE TO go to the bathroom," Heidi whined, shifting in her seat and pulling on the seat harness in her agitation.

She restlessly tugged on her bright copper hair, which Syd had woven into a braid that morning while trying to monitor Jamie brushing his teeth at the same time. The small tan dog cradled in the little girl's arms was madly scrambling for freedom. The dog finally gained his emancipation and hopped onto the seat, where another dog lay snoozing by Jamie's leg.

"Are we gonna eat soon?" Jamie piped up, crawling onto his knees and looking over the back of the seat at his aunt as she stashed spandex pants, fake-fur jacket and wig in a bag. His dark brown eyes, the same puppy-dog color as his mother's eyes, watched his aunt with great interest.

From the first time she'd seen her niece and nephew as babies, Syd couldn't help but notice how each child was a mirror image of one of their parents. Tiny Heidi looked like her father and aunt with the bright red hair, faint freckles sprinkled across the nose and eyes a brilliant blue lapis. Although, Syd resolutely denied having the stubborn streak the little girl already displayed. Jamie, with his ash-blond hair and dark brown eyes, had his scientist mother's serious demeanor, and at nine years of age had the ability to take a major problem and turn it into a minor one. Syd once declared he could argue with the concise manner of a seasoned trial attorney. No wonder there were days she looked at them and felt scared to death at the idea of having their lives in her hands.

"In a few minutes," she assured him, pulling a fisherman-knit sweater over her head. She looked in a mirror as she creamed off the heavy makeup.

"Why are you always doing somethin' to make you look different?" Jamie asked, picking up the blond wig and plopping it on his head. Heidi giggled as he turned to her and made faces.

"Because this way it won't be easy for Mean Mr. Leo to find us." She plucked the wig off his head and stuffed it in the bag next to her clothing.

As she pulled a navy knit cap on top of her head, Syd thought about the man she'd encountered in the convenience store.

Tall and dark-haired, with chiseled features, green eyes that looked deceptively sleepy and an aura surrounding a rugged demeanor that spelled danger with a capital *D*. She idly wondered how he had broken his nose. She wouldn't be surprised if an angry husband had done that! He was the type of man she'd do well to stay far away from because the danger could be to herself.

"Probably a redneck who has visions of body slamming with a hot blonde in the back of his battered pickup, which undoubtedly has a gun rack in the cab," she muttered, closing the back of the truck and walking around to the driver's door. She looked at the two children. "Okay, kids, what shall we feast on tonight? Hamburgers, fish and chips, or pizza?"

"Hamburgers!" Heidi shouted.

"Pizza!" Jamie yelled with equal fervor.

"Something tells me I'm not choosing healthy menus for you guys." Syd drove around from the back of the gas station where she'd made her quick change of clothing from party girl to fresh-faced ex-government agent. "Let's get some dinner, then I'll pick up some groceries before we head for the cabin Uncle Joey arranged for us to stay in."

"If we go there, how will Santa Claus find us?" Heidi asked. Syd and Jamie had been hearing the same question from Heidi for the past six days during their roundabout route from Virginia to Tahoe, California. "He knows I live at 337 Zinnia Lane," she announced with the self-importance of a small child who has memorized her address. "But he doesn't know I'll be here."

"It doesn't matter!" Jamie told her. "Because Santa isn't re—"

"Santa always knows where we are, honey," Syd smoothly inserted, giving her nephew a warning look. "He won't have any trouble finding you."

"I hope so," she said with a worried downturn of her mouth. "I don't want him to give my Talking Taffy doll to somebody else."

Syd made a mental note to make sure the doll was still well secured in a hidden compartment in the truck. She was determined to give the kids the kind of Christmas they deserved. While she couldn't bring back their parents, she could give them a joyous holiday.

"If we have hamburgers for dinner tonight, can we have pizza tomorrow night?" Jamie asked.

Syd smiled and touched his cheek. "That's very nice of you," she said softly.

He wiggled around in the seat. "Yeah, well, she's little. When she doesn't get her way, she yells real loud."

"Maybe this mom business won't be so bad after all," Syd murmured, turning the Jeep toward downtown Tahoe and its variety of fast-food restaurants.

"You forgot to take me to the bathroom! And I have to go *now!*" Heidi suddenly shrieked loud enough to shatter glass.

Syd jerked the steering wheel to one side for an illegal U-turn. "Then again, maybe I should rethink my confidence level."

As she drove, she snapped upward glances in the rearview mirror every few minutes for signs of any vehicle that might be following them. She doubted Leo could have tracked her down so quickly, but she knew better than to underestimate her superior. While the town was well known for its gambling casinos and ski slopes, it wasn't known as one of her hangouts when she was in the United States. Which was why she considered the area a suitable hideout for her and the kids. She needed the time to figure out what she was going to do with her life, and she didn't want Leo's input.

As Syd drove back toward the gas station, she thought she saw the same dark green four-wheel-drive vehicle she'd spied in the convenience market's parking lot. Until she saw another one, then another. It appeared they were the vehicle of choice for Tahoe residents and visitors alike.

"*Bathroom!*" Heidi spat out the word in the demanding tone only a five-year-old girl could accomplish.

Syd pressed the accelerator to the floor. "Hold it for five seconds more!"

She skidded to a stop in front of the gas station, pulled Heidi out of the truck and ran inside for the key. As she hustled Heidi into the bathroom and listened to the little girl complain it smelled bad, she decided motherhood wasn't anything like the storylines on the television sitcoms.

KI DROVE UP THE STEEP road that led to the mountaintop cabin he owned along with his three friends. Once a year, he, Steve, Tripp and Deke would head up here for their time to unwind. A two-story A-frame with lots of glass front and back and an upper deck surrounding the building, it looked like heaven to his weary mind. He parked his truck in the rear, and after unlocking the door and shutting off the alarm system, he began unloading his things. After the punishing drive he'd made to get to Tahoe, he was more than ready to sit back and relax in front of the fire with a beer. But he knew he wanted the truck unloaded before it started to get dark.

Ki made short work of carrying his suitcase and duffel bag inside. He'd carry them upstairs to his room later. He carefully placed his laptop computer on a side table where it would be out of sight, since he didn't intend to get back to work until the next morning.

After he unloaded the groceries and stashed them away in cupboards, he zapped a frozen dinner in the microwave, then settled down on the couch with a bottle of beer and a plastic tray of lasagna. A Rolling Stones CD played softly in the background.

''Relax,'' he intoned, eating half his dinner and pushing the rest of it away. He leaned back and propped his stockinged feet on the coffee table as he cradled a bottle of beer in his lap. He stared into the fireplace, listening to the fire crackle in the room's silence. "You came here to get your mind back on murder and mayhem. So do it."

Except, Ki silently lamented as he tipped the beer bottle to his lips, that was the last thing he wanted to do. Meeting Thomas Baskin had sowed some very unsettling seeds in his mind. He thought back to the months he'd spent near the Illinois State Penitentiary.

The man wasn't the human nightmare the media had made him out to be. He'd turned out to be much worse.

When Ki was ushered into the room to interview the convicted murderer, he had expected Baskin to be good-looking, articulate and charming. After all, there were plenty of newspaper pictures of the man. His looks and charm had helped him lead almost twenty women into his deadly web of deceit. And he would have continued his rampage if his last victim hadn't remained alive long enough to talk to the authorities.

As Ki spent weeks talking to Thomas, trying to find out his reasons for what he did, Ki started questioning himself. Thomas seduced women. Ki seduced his readers. He hated the similarity.

After the first few days of hearing the man's lethal alternatives for divorce, Ki broke up with a stockbroker he'd been seeing for several months and instead spent his nights pacing the small apartment he'd rented. When he tried to sleep, he had nightmares about men who hated women so much they killed them and tried to use the name of love for their excuse.

"I enjoy women," Thomas had told Ki during that first week of interviews. From the beginning he had been remarkably candid with the writer. "I enjoy looking at them, talking to them and making love with them. I also feel I should offer them a commitment. Marrying them gives them the security they need. That's what makes them happy."

"And marrying them gives you access to their bank accounts." Ki spoke in the neutral tone he always adopted with his subjects.

Thomas's shrug was unapologetic. "I loved them all, but I knew the time would come when they would want to leave me. I made sure they didn't."

"Why would they leave you if they loved you so much? Why did you continue to do something that has such dire consequences? You had to know you'd get caught eventually." Ki gestured to the barred windows and the burly guard standing nearby. "Is this how you want to spend the rest of your life?"

His reply was simple. "Being sent here meant I made a mistake and I have to pay for it. But I can't fault Felice for that. No matter what, I gave my ladies whatever they needed. I see nothing wrong in what I did, and I mourn their passing because I truly loved each one. And with their deaths, I was always assured of their love for me."

Ki thought of the pain some of the women had endured before they died by Baskin's hand. For a man who claimed to love his wives, he hadn't found pleasant ways of killing them. Two women had been bludgeoned to death. Thomas's original statement to the police had been the assumption of a break-in and that the woman had caught a burglar. And the last had been scalded to death. Since each time he bore a different name and a supposedly airtight alibi, the police had no reason to suspect him. Until his last wife's accident took a turn Thomas hadn't anticipated.

After his arrest and background checks were accomplished, it was soon learned that Thomas Baskin, aka Tommy Baker, aka Baxter Thomas and so on had been married and widowed at least seventeen times. Even Thomas couldn't give an accurate count of how many women he had married and murdered over the last twenty-odd years. But Ki had the list. With prodding and pushing, he got more information than he could use. And he discovered just how deadly charm can be.

Ki sipped the beer from the bottle, savoring the cold, yeasty flavor trickling down his throat. That was when he looked across the room and realized he hadn't put his laptop computer as far out of sight as he'd thought. It sat there as if in silent accusation. *Finish the book!*

He muttered a pithy curse and levered himself off the couch.

"Go ahead and sit around feeling sorry for yourself while you get drunk, old man," he muttered, stalking into the kitchen and pulling another bottle of beer out of the refrigerator.

As Ki sprawled on the couch, he suddenly realized this was the first time he'd been at the cabin by himself. It felt odd. He, Steve, Tripp and Deke always came up here together for their kick-back time. They'd drink beer, play pool and shoot the bull.

"And now Steve and Tripp are married." He stared morosely at the bottle cradled between his palms.

"Hell, for all I know, Deke will be next. What's the world coming to when four guys can't happily remain single? Good thing I don't have to worry about a woman snaring me."

By the time the beer had sufficiently dulled his senses, it was close to midnight. Ki was hazily aware he wasn't in any shape to make it upstairs. He opted for stumbling into the downstairs bedroom and dropping onto the bed, where he instantly fell into an alcohol-induced sleep.

"I NEVER GET LOST," Syd muttered, peering through the windshield at the shadowy outline of an A-frame mountain cabin up a fairly steep hill. She was glad for the four-wheel drive capability as she started up the hill. "I always have a perfect sense of direction. I was left in the middle of miles of underground crypts and found my way out. It was Matt's map that screwed me up."

She cursed the map her friend had given her and cursed her friend at the same time.

"You're not supposed to say bad words," Jamie said sleepily from the back seat where he lay curled up under a quilt.

"I didn't say any bad words."

"Yes, you did."

"So when did you learn to speak Chinese?"

"I don't have to speak it to know you said bad words. You always say 'em in another language. Are we there yet?"

Syd braked to a stop by the front door. She knew better than to try to reason with Jamie. His ready answers were always so logical. "Yes, we're there."

"How come we got here so late?" Jamie was sleepy and cranky.

"It had something to do with Heidi taking so long with her dinner and our taking in two movies," she replied, shutting off the engine. She reached over the seat and gently shook Heidi's knee. "Hey, sweetie, up and at 'em," she said in a low voice.

Heidi mumbled a few grumpy words and pushed Syd's hand away.

"Help her out of her seat," Syd instructed as she climbed out of the truck, digging through her jeans pocket for the house key that had been sent to her. "We'll get inside, then I'll come back for the dogs." She ordered the two dogs to stay put as she climbed out.

Syd didn't bother to turn on the lights as she pushed the door open farther and waited for the two children to follow.

"Bathroom," Heidi said sleepily.

"Sometimes I think that's the only word you know," Syd mumbled.

"I don't have to take her, do I?" Jamie grumbled, even as Heidi tugged on his hand, pulling him in the general direction of the rear of the house.

Syd grew very still. They weren't alone in the house. She didn't need to hear strange footsteps or voices to know that. Her sixth sense was more than enough to warn her.

She moved stealthily through the dark room, keeping all her senses open. She was intent on getting to the kids and getting them out of there fast.

Syd knew the other person was there mere seconds before she was jumped. She reacted with split-second timing. She spun around, her hands and raised foot ready to deflect an attack. Her first blow met a bare, rock-hard stomach.

The man's breath whooshed out of his diaphragm and his muttered curse told her she had achieved her goal. But that didn't stop him from rushing forward. If Syd hadn't jumped back instinctively, she would have been crushed beneath the man's body.

She fought back, not pausing until she had her attacker pinned to the floor. It wasn't until she straddled his body and her hands found nothing but bare skin that she realized his bottom half was as bare as his top half.

"Auntie Syd!"

"Get out of here, Jamie!" she shouted, but her warning was too late. The little boy had already turned on a lamp.

Syd stared at the face of the man she had seen in the convenience store earlier that day. He stared back at her in equal shock. She started to shift, then realized just exactly where she was straddling him and that a wide-eyed Heidi was staring at more of this stranger than a little girl should.

"Jamie, take Heidi into the kitchen," she ordered, keeping her gaze fastened on the man's face, although she had to admit she'd grown even more aware of the body beneath her.

"That man isn't wearing any clothes," Heidi piped up as her brother pulled her none too gently by the hand.

"Yeah, well, Auntie Syd will take care of him before he knows what hit him," he replied, dragging her out of the room.

"I'll get up nice and easy and so will you," Syd told Ki in a level voice. "Just in case you haven't figured it out yet, I can take you down any time, so don't try anything."

He held his hands up. "No problem. Just be gentle with me."

Ki watched her straighten up with feline grace. He'd recognized the bright blue eyes. The same watchful gaze he'd noticed earlier was there as he took his time standing up and nonchalantly reached for a blanket to wrap around his waist. He was pleased to notice her covert glance downward as he covered himself up. He turned his head at the sound of dogs barking and wondered what other surprises the lady had in store for him.

"What happened to the Scarlett O'Hara drawl and the Dolly Parton hair?"

"This house is private property. What are you doing here?"

He appreciated the way she smoothly deflected his question. But that method never stopped him before. Hell, he'd used it countless times himself!

"I own one-fourth of this place. What's your excuse?"

Chapter Two

Syd determinedly kept her gaze centered on his face and not on the broad expanse of hair-covered chest or lower on the blanket that slipped downward each time he took a breath. When caught in a difficult situation, she always believed in remaining on the offensive. This was no exception.

"None of the owners use the cabin this time of year."

Ki crossed his arms in front of his chest and studied Syd with a slow, sweeping gaze. Their fight had sent her knit cap slipping partway off her head, sending strands of red hair floating down to just above her shoulders. While her eyes were still that potent color of blue, the heavy makeup was gone, leaving her skin a translucent pearl color, and faint freckles were now visible across her nose. With a heavy knit sweater hanging loosely around her hips, leg-hugging jeans and boots, her curves weren't as evident.

"This isn't a time-share, sweetheart," he drawled. "So why don't you tell me why you and the Dead End kids were breaking into my house?"

"If you're one of the owners, it's only one-fourth your house," she corrected him with a smirk, "and we've been invited to stay here."

"By whom?"

"Steve Chambliss."

Ki looked her over again. "How do you know Steve?"

"I don't, but a friend of his arranged this for us. He said there wouldn't be any problem in our staying here." Syd hated to make explanations, especially to men who looked comfortable wearing nothing more than a blanket while she had the good fortune to remember what he looked like without it. "I know that the house is jointly owned by Steve, Tripp Ashby, Ki Jones and Deke Washburn. They've been buddies who go all the way back to their hell-raising days at Beckett College. Now, if you don't mind, I have two very tired children who need to be in bed." She cocked her head as she heard the frenzied barking from the front of the house. "And two very upset dogs who probably want to find the nearest tree."

Ki held up his hand like a crossing guard halting further words. Although he had to admit, sparring with this woman was the most fun he'd had in quite a while. "Well, lady, you've just met up with Ukiah Jones, and the last thing I want around here are kids and dogs. I'm out here for peace and quiet, not to listen to kids whine and cry and whatever else they do and to have dogs tearing up furniture and peeing on the carpet. You'll have to find another place. Take my advice. When you start looking, wear the blue spandex. I'm sure you'll find a room in no time."

Syd's jaw tightened as she concentrated on tamping down her fury at his callous disregard for her charges. "Do you realize what time it is?"

"Hey, sweetheart, I don't care what time it is. I wasn't the one who broke in here!"

She advanced on him with anger radiating out of every pore in her body. Every bone fairly quivered with fury. Anyone who had worked with her in the past would have been surprised, since she was always known for her cool composure in the line of fire.

"I didn't break in! I was given a damn key!"

"Auntie Syd, you said a bad word again!" Jamie's voice rang out from the kitchen.

"Syd?" Ki arched an eyebrow. Humor curved his lips upward. "Well, Syd, we have a problem here. And you're it."

She was used to figuring her options in fractions of a second. The way she looked at it, this was one of those times when she needed all her wits about her. She always stood her ground, never backed down and never took prisoners.

"Not really. It's very simple. You stay in your one-fourth of the house. We'll stay in Steve's fourth."

"You don't understand. I came up here for peace and quiet so I could work. Your being around means I won't get either. Why did you come up here?"

Syd wasn't about to trust a stranger, even a good-looking one.

"The children lost their parents recently," she said in a low voice. "I'm now their legal guardian and wanted to give them a change of scenery."

"What about the mutts? They lose their mommy and daddy, too? Give me a break. Sob stories don't cut with me. You're going to have to come up with something a lot better than that."

Syd sifted through the little information she had about the other three owners. "Yeah, you're Ukiah Jones. I understand he's the cynical one. Aren't you supposed to be in Chicago?"

Ki didn't like it when strangers knew his itinerary. Especially mouthy ones with beautiful eyes. He started to say something pithy when movement in the back of the room caught his attention. He looked beyond Syd's shoulder to the two children standing under the archway leading to the kitchen. The boy held his sister's hand tightly and moved closer to her, as if to protect her. Ki closed his mouth, then opened it again, but nothing came out.

"All right, you can stay tonight. It's too late for you to find a motel room, anyway," he conceded wearily. "But you have to go in the morning."

Syd was an expert on when to speak and when to remain silent. This was most definitely the time to remain silent. She settled for nodding.

"You can use two of the bedrooms upstairs," Ki said with a small sigh, waving his hand upward.

"Thank you." The words burned in her throat. After all, she had as much right to be here as he did, even if he did own one-fourth of the cabin. She quickly headed for the door.

"I'm sure you'll understand my not offering to help you carry in your luggage," Ki said mockingly.

Syd turned around and offered him an equally mocking smile. "Don't worry about it, Mr. Jones. I'd hate to think of you freezing ... yourself."

She pulled suitcases out of the back while the dogs ran around and left their marks on the moonlit snow.

"Come on, guys," she called out to them and waited for them to run into the house.

"Are we staying here with the bad man?" Heidi asked in her piping voice.

Unknown to them, Ki stood inside his bedroom, wincing as he heard the little girl's question.

"Yes, sweetie, but don't worry, Auntie Syd will protect you." She swept the girl up in her arms and tickled her tummy. Heidi squealed with laughter. "All right, time for bed. Come on, Cocoa, Bogie, bedtime," she called to the dogs as they climbed the stairs.

Ki lay in bed hearing muffled sounds overhead as the trio readied themselves for bed. He could hear chatter between the boy and girl, water running in the bathroom and eventually blessed silence.

"Oh, hell," he muttered, rolling over and punching his pillow with his fist. "I should have stayed in Chicago."

He finally fell asleep but the image of brilliant blue eyes followed him into his dreams.

SYD SHOULD HAVE BEEN used to sharing her bed with two dogs and occasionally a little girl, but tonight was different. She was so tired from days of keeping watch over her shoulder, of constant disguises and name changes so Leo wouldn't have an easy time of tracking her down, that she felt as if she could sleep through a nuclear war.

She shivered under the cold sheets as Bogie, her half Chihuahua, half terrier, stretched out beside her under the covers in search of body heat. Cocoa, her half terrier and half poodle, lay on top of the covers curled up next to her rear end. She wondered how long it would take before Heidi showed up with her battered teddy bear in tow.

Every time she closed her eyes, pictures of a naked Ki flashed through her brain. A potent reminder of how long it had been since she'd been with a man who sent her senses reeling. If, in fact, any man had ever affected her the way Ukiah Jones did. And for a woman in her business—correction, ex-business— anything that threw off her sense of self-protection could prove to be dangerous.

"Auntie Syd."

She opened her eyes and turned her head. Heidi, wearing a flannel nightgown with a cartoon portrait of Aladdin and Princess Jasmine on the front, stood by the side of the bed. A dark brown teddy bear dangled from one hand.

"My bed is making funny noises," she mumbled, rubbing her eyes with a tiny fist. "Can I sleep with you?"

Syd smiled and pulled the covers back. "Come on in, sweetie." After the little girl was warmly covered, she curved her arm around Heidi's shoulders. "Is Jamie still asleep?"

"Uh-huh."

When they first got ready for bed an hour ago, Heidi had insisted on sleeping with her brother. Syd knew it wouldn't last. She hadn't been insisting on Heidi sleeping in her own bed, because she knew the little girl needed a major dose of TLC. Luckily, that was something she was capable of giving. A low growl from her other side vibrated through her leg as she shifted and almost crushed Bogie. She soothed the small dog as Heidi buried her face in Syd's shoulder.

"Are we ever gonna go home?" Heidi whispered.

Syd thought of the lovely home Shane and Jenny had fixed up for their growing family. Shane had set up a swing set and slide in the backyard along with a swimming pool, because Jamie had proved to be a little fish. Shane used to brag his son would grow up to be an Olympic gold medal winner. She mourned he'd never even see his son grow up.

"Soon," she replied, brushing Heidi's bangs away from her face. "Now, go to sleep."

"That mean man isn't going to let us stay here, is he?"

"You let Auntie Syd handle him, okay?"

Heidi let loose a sleepy giggle. "Then I guess we're stayin'."

Syd had to smile. Her tiny niece had so much faith in her that she knew she couldn't let her down. She closed her eyes and thought about her upcoming bout with a man with the most beautiful green eyes she'd ever seen.

KI WAS HAVING the best dream he'd had in years. A gorgeous woman wearing only a fur coat over a luscious naked body was in his arms, planting wet kisses all over his face. His smile broadened as he thought about the erotic things he'd let her do to him before he returned the favor.

"Hey, honey, don't worry, we've got all night," he mumbled, wrapping his arms around her. "And I sure don't intend to rush when it's my turn."

Her whimpers of delight echoed in his ear as he laughed and pulled her toward him for a kiss. A kiss totally unlike any kiss he'd ever received. She seemed to lap him up.

Ki rose swiftly through the cotton wool of sleep and forced his eyes open. Instead of the beautiful woman in his arms, he found a dark brown dog lying squarely on his chest. He picked the dog up and stared at him.

"Hell, you're not even a female," he grumbled, putting the dog to one side.

The dog whimpered and pawed at him. His large brown eyes signaled a distress that even Ki could understand.

"Don't tell me you have to go out?" The dog's ears immediately pricked up.

"Ah, hell," Ki muttered, pushing the covers aside and swinging his legs out of bed. He quickly pulled on a pair of sweatpants and sweatshirt. "Come on." He gestured for the dog to follow him.

He swore under his breath as a blast of cold air hit him when he opened the back door. The dog ran outside and headed for the nearest tree. He only stayed out long enough to do his business before running back inside. He barked his pleasure and ran circles around Ki's legs.

"Uh-uh, you want anything else, you can go ask your screwy mistress."

"Cocoa's always like that after he's gone potty."

Ki looked up to see the boy standing in the kitchen doorway. While his red flannel pajamas looked warm enough, his feet were bare and he stood on the tile floor with one foot propped on the other.

"Shouldn't you be wearing slippers or socks or something?" He pulled a bag of coffee beans out of the freezer and dug the coffee grinder out of a cabinet. There were few things Ki was selective about. Coffee was one of them. He bought whole beans and ground them fresh every morning.

"I'm sorry Cocoa woke you up. I guess he had to go really bad and couldn't wake Auntie Syd up. She was really tired last night. Auntie Syd said we aren't supposed to bug you, but I guess Cocoa didn't understand. He just does what he wants."

"Just like his mistress," Ki muttered.

Jamie sidled into the kitchen and perched on a nearby stool, watching Ki's movements with a gaze Ki felt was too solemn for a boy so young. He reached down and patted Cocoa's head. The dog nuzzled his hand and left the room.

"What are you doing?"

"Making coffee." Ki set up the coffeemaker with quick, efficient movements.

"Dad used to do it that way. He's dead. So's our mom."

Ki's hand stilled over the coffeemaker's switch. "Yeah, I thought maybe that was the case."

"Heidi doesn't understand what it means. She's only five," he pronounced with the arrogance of a mature nine-year-old. "She thinks they're off on a vacation or something, so Auntie Syd's gonna take care of us now. Although Dad said Auntie Syd's idea of taking care of anybody is pretty iffy. They were twins, so he always said if anybody could say anything they wanted about her it was him. He also said she's got a James Bond complex." He paused. "Whatever that means."

Ki hid his smile. It looked as if this kid was the best one to pump about his dear "Auntie Syd."

"What's your name, kid?"

Jamie held out his hand in an adult manner. "James Allen Taylor, but everyone calls me Jamie. I was named after my grandfather. My sister's Heidi Elizabeth Taylor. I don't think she was named after anybody."

Ki swallowed another smile as he put together the various names. "I'm pleased to meet you, James Taylor." He shook Jamie's hand. "What about your Auntie Syd? Who was she named after?"

Jamie squirmed uneasily on his perch. "We're not really supposed to talk about her."

That was new. He wondered if that meant she was as crazy as she seemed last night.

"Yeah, well, I've got relatives I'm not supposed to talk about, either."

"It's just because Auntie Syd's a spy," Jamie explained, clearly not remembering exactly what he was and wasn't supposed to say about her.

Ki chalked that statement right up there with his great aunt who used to believe little green men came down to talk to her once a month. He turned to see Jamie casting a yearning look toward the refrigerator. It brought memories of himself at Jamie's age, when hunger was a constant fact of life.

"You want some breakfast?" He opened the refrigerator and pulled out a plastic bottle of orange juice.

Jamie's head bobbed up and down. "Auntie Syd took us to McDonald's for breakfast yesterday. I told her Mom always said a person'd be better off eating lard, but Auntie Syd said it was better than eating worms. Heidi started screaming that our food had worms in it, and we had to get out of there fast 'cause people were looking at us real funny. And I don't mean the kind of funny where somebody laughs."

Ki coughed to cover his chuckle as he poured a glass of juice and handed it to Jamie. "Son, you've got a pretty strange family. Are the dogs at least halfway normal?"

"They're Auntie Syd's," he replied, as if that explained it all. "She got Cocoa when he was a puppy when she was first back here and later on she decided he needed company. She said Bogie picked her out the same way Cocoa chose her. She said since she had been thinking of staying all the time, she was glad she had the dogs."

"Bogie?" he frowned, pouring himself a glass of juice. "After Humphrey Bogart?"

"Amazing how everyone thinks that." Syd wandered into the kitchen with the small tan dog on her heels and Heidi and Cocoa not far behind.

Heidi dragged a teddy bear after her. She wore a heavy quilted robe over her pajamas and pink bunny slippers. Syd was dressed in black knit leggings and a forest green wool sweater that stopped just below her waist. Ki uneasily noticed that the wide neckline seemed to have a habit of sliding off one creamy shoulder as she moved. She'd looped her hair up on top of her head, although wisps escaped to caress her nape and cheeks. She didn't wear any makeup and didn't need any to accentuate her brilliantly colored eyes. What had Ki's nerve endings quivering with lust was the most haunting fragrance emanating from her skin. What was she wearing? Sex Potion Number Nine?

"Maybe it's because I never heard of a dog named after a golf term."

"Neither have I, but if it's that important for you to know, Bogie was named after a radar blip," she said in a haughty voice that Ki decided could easily grate on his nerves.

He shook his head as if he wasn't sure he heard correctly. "A radar blip?"

"You know, those little blips on a radar screen that aren't really there," she went on as if he should be able to understand something that was so clear in her own mind. "The name seemed to suit him." She unerringly headed for the cabinet that held glasses. She gestured for Heidi to sit down while she poured the juice into a glass. "I figure the least I can do is cook breakfast for everyone." She opened the refrigerator door. "Ham and eggs sound all right?" As she gathered up the ingredients, she paused long enough to pour herself a cup of coffee. She breathed in the aroma before sipping. "Very good. French vanilla, isn't it?"

He nodded. "Anything else you want to take of mine?"

She found a pan and began cracking the eggs. "Not just yet. Jamie, would you put Bogie out, please?"

The tiny dog danced on his hind legs, pressing his paws against the door as if he could push it open himself. He raced outside the moment Jamie opened it.

"What the hell kind of dog is that?"

"I call him a terri-chui. Half terrier, half Chihuahua. Cocoa, that's c-o-c-o-a by the way, is half poodle and half terrier. Although there are days when I think they're both more terrorist than terrier."

"What ever happened to traditional dog names like Fluffy or Spot or Pancho?"

Syd looked over her shoulder with a steady gaze. "I don't believe in tradition."

Ki leaned against the counter and sipped his coffee, deciding it wasn't so bad watching someone else cook. Especially when that someone else wore an errant sweater that kept dropping off her shoulder.

"That's easy to see. So how come you're all the way out here when you should be home for Christmas setting out milk and cookies for Santa Claus?"

"Auntie Syd said Santa could find us here!" Heidi suddenly erupted in an earsplitting screech. "Santa has to know where I am so he can bring me my Talking Taffy doll!''

Ki wiggled a forefinger in his ear to make sure it was still in working order. "Does she come with a volume control?" he muttered.

"Santa knows where you are, Heidi," Syd calmly assured her as she sent Ki a warning look. "And he'll be here Christmas Eve night."

"The kids have accents that don't belong to California," Ki went on as he delicately probed for information. "I'd say back East. Right?"

"Last I heard native Californians were a distinct minority." Syd chopped ham into small cubes and added it to the egg mixture, then began chopping cheese into tiny pieces. "Kids, why don't you go on up and get dressed before you eat?"

"That means she doesn't want us to hear what she's going to say," Jamie groused, climbing off the stool and grabbing Heidi's hand. "Come on."

Ki turned to the scratching sounds coming from the door. Syd opened it, laughing as the light-tan-colored dog jumped into her arms.

"Poor baby, you must be freezing," she cooed, rubbing his sides with her hands. "I'd better get one of your sweaters out for you next time." When she returned to the stove, both dogs hovered by her legs, obviously looking for handouts.

Ki was grateful to notice she washed her hands before she picked up food. While he didn't adhere to proper hygiene when he did his own cooking, he drew the line at someone else hauling around a dog then not washing those same hands before handling his food.

Although he might draw not the line if she held on to
the dog and that sweater slipped off her shoulder even
more.

"Jamie said their parents are dead."

Her movements paused. "Yes, they are. I told you
that last night."

"He also said his dad was your twin."

Her head bobbed in an abrupt nod.

Ki sensed her pain even as she seemed to refuse to
admit it.

"I've read that twins share a bond no other sibling
could understand."

Syd turned around. "We hadn't seen much of each
other in the last few years, but I knew to the second
when he died because a part of me died at the same
time. I gather that's what you mean. He and his wife
were killed by a strung-out druggie who wanted their
money. It took the authorities two weeks to track me
down." All because of her plans changing when she
was on the trail of that agent in Lisbon. "By the time
I got back, they had already been buried and the kids
were in foster care because we had no other family to
take care of them. Heidi refused to talk to anyone and
Jamie's way of coping was to fight anyone and everyone who dared to approach him. I wanted them away
from familiar surroundings so they could have a
chance to heal."

Ki never considered himself a sucker. He never
loaned money or his car, or believed a sob story. But
there was something about those eyes and steady gaze
that did something to him. Not to mention the kids.
He again wished he'd stayed in Chicago.

"I came here for peace and quiet," he said without preamble. "I have work to do and I don't like interruptions. Can you promise me that I'll get peace and quiet with all of you here?"

"No," she said honestly. "But I can promise that I'll do the cooking, although I'll warn you I'm not exactly the best. And I'll keep the kids out of your way as much as possible. All I ask is that you don't advertise our presence."

Ki burst out laughing. "Advertise your presence? Lady, you sound like a covert agent."

Syd looked down at Bogie who leaned against her leg. "Nothing unusual about that. I sound like a lot of people."

"Actress?" he inquired.

She smiled. She waved a spatula in time to her words. "Role-playing is very therapeutic, don't you think? It makes a person feel as if they can be anyone they want. Whether they want to be an astronaut or a cowboy or a fireman."

"Or spy?"

"Or spy," she cheerfully echoed. "Didn't you ever want to be James Bond when you grew up?"

"I was more into the 'The Addams Family,' myself. I thought Morticia was pretty hot stuff."

Syd cocked her head to one side as she considered his statement. "So you're into tall and slinky?"

"No, I just go nuts when a woman speaks French." Ki walked over and looked into the pan where fluffy scrambled eggs with bits of ham and melted cheese resided. He pinched off a bit of egg and threw it into his mouth. "This isn't bad at all."

"Of course not. Breakfast is my favorite meal, so I tend to go all out when I'm making it."

Although Ki's attention was fixed on her, and as far as he knew she hadn't budged a fraction of an inch, he would swear she had made sure she stayed out of his range. He moved closer, ignoring the growl from below. He dismissed the small dog as harmless.

"Don't worry, honey," he said, growling a little himself as he leaned over and murmured in her ear, "I won't bite."

She looked amused instead of alarmed by his provocative statement. "I'm surprised you couldn't come up with a more original line."

"Maybe so, but how many men can also assure you they haven't had to wear a muzzle in years?"

Chapter Three

Syd was grateful Heidi and Jamie appeared on the scene before she seriously thought about responding to Ki's tantalizing statement in kind. After all, she never turned down a dare and Ki had thrown out an interesting one.

The children also saved Syd from going insane and throwing Ki to the ground. What she'd have done after she had him in a prone position would have depended on Ki. She had an idea that he wouldn't have resisted. She settled for a smile that would have done the sultriest feline proud and leaned forward to trail the back of her fingers down his cheek.

"That's reassuring to hear," she said in a husky voice that brought to Ki's mind thoughts of candle-light, bluesy jazz on the stereo, secluded bedrooms and soft beds. "Let me comfort you with the news that I've always kept my shots up-to-date. Now, why don't you pop some bread into the toaster and get out plates and silverware while I dish up our breakfast."

His green eyes darkened with deep emerald fire before he turned away and found the requested items.

"What a novelty," he commented, handing her four dishes and carrying the silverware over to the breakfast nook that looked over the rear yard.

"What? Having breakfast?"

"No, that's nothing new. But having breakfast with a woman I didn't sleep with the night before is."

Syd prided herself on keeping cool in the most dangerous situations. She faced guns without turning a hair and once disarmed a bomb with seconds to go without fumbling. She reminded herself that if she could face some of the meanest most dangerous criminals in the world, she could handle Ukiah Jones. As long as she kept her hormones under control.

"Is breakfast ready?" Jamie ran into the kitchen, skidding to a stop beside Syd just as she picked up two of the plates.

"Yes, it is, bottomless pit. Have a seat." Syd set the plates on the table. Before she could retrieve the other two, Ki had already brought them over.

Heidi watched Ki with a wide curious gaze. "Don'cha have to get out of your pajamas, too?"

"Oh, these aren't my—" he bit off the explanation that he didn't wear anything to bed. "No, these are my lying around the house clothes."

"Why do you lie around the house?"

"It's just an expression, honey," Syd told her. "Mr. Jones works out of his home."

Heidi turned to Ki. "How do you work at home? Daddy always goes away every morning to his office. So does Mommy."

Syd's face tightened at Heidi's mention of her father in the present tense, but she remained silent. She applied herself to dropping two more bread slices in the toaster while buttering the ones already done and slicing them in halves.

"Shane was a graphic artist with a large advertising firm. He used to boast that he could make even cod liver oil look good. Jenny was the saner member of the family. She was a microbiologist," she said quietly, setting the plate down and sitting down herself.

That was when Ki noticed four small bowls in one corner of the kitchen. Two filled with water and two in which both dogs had their noses buried in kibble. He slowly turned to Syd. His expression said it all. He was not pleased with her attempt to make him feel sorry enough for them that he'd let them stay.

"They have to eat, too," she calmly explained, forking up eggs and lifting them to her lips. "Eat your food before it gets cold."

"You're not my mother," he groused even as he did just that, much to Syd's amusement.

"She's not our mom, either, but we do what she says," Jamie explained. "Because she knows really gross ways to make us behave."

"Really gross, huh?" He looked at Syd. "What really gross methods do you use?"

"Oh, the usual," she said airily, looking at her charges with love-warmed eyes. She glanced at Ki, lowering her voice. "I am talking tortures so horrifying that if I told you about them you would never be the same again."

"She always says that!" Jamie declared with a disgusted snort. He finished his juice in one gulp, picked up his plate and silverware and carried it over to the counter. "Can I go outside?"

"I want to go, too!" Heidi jumped up and down.

Syd hesitated.

"There's nothing around here they can hurt," Ki assured her.

"All right, but put on your coats and boots," she told them. "Jamie, keep an eye on your sister. Both of you, stay close to the cabin where I can still see you."

"I know, I know. Don't push her into any snowbanks," Jamie muttered, walking with heavy steps as he left the kitchen with Heidi fast on his heels. "Don't tie her to any trees and don't try to sell her to anybody by saying she was left under a bush."

Now Ki knew just how limited his exposure to children was. "Are you sure he's not a thirty-year-old man in a kid's body?"

"We all have wondered that from the time he started to talk," she replied, getting up to pour herself more coffee and holding up the pot to see if Ki wanted more. When he nodded, she brought the pot over to the table and filled his cup. "Then he does something that's totally in keeping with his age, as if he's reassuring people he's a kid after all."

"Not many single women would be willing to take on two kids," he commented.

"Jamie and Heidi are very easy to take."

"Tie my hood," Heidi demanded, waddling over to Syd. With a hooded parka and heavy pants, she resembled a bright pink duckling.

Syd held up her hands, wiggling her fingers. "What's the magic word?"

"Please." Heidi's smile was like a sunbeam.

Syd looped the cord into a bow and double-knotted it. "There, now you're all safe from falling snow angels," she told her, giving her a big hug.

The little girl giggled. "That's silly. There aren't any falling snow angels."

Syd dropped a kiss on her forehead. "Oh, yes, there are. They just keep out of sight and fall on you when you least expect it."

"Can we go out now?" Jamie queried in a long-suffering tone.

"Yes, just don't—"

"Go near the Jeep. We know." He grabbed his sister's hand and dragged her out.

"Why should they stay away from your truck?"

"I don't want them to set off the alarm," she explained, picking up plates.

"I don't think you need to worry about anyone showing up and stealing your truck way out here." Ki picked up his plates. "You cooked. It's only fair I clean up."

"How does a man get the name Ukiah?" she asked curiously. "Is it a family name or what?"

"It's a family name if he was conceived in the back of his daddy's Chevy in the town of Ukiah, California, and his momma, who doesn't possess an ounce of imagination, decided it would be a fitting name."

Syd's gaze softened. "Your dad took off?"

"The minute he heard the results of the pregnancy test." He shrugged. "No big loss from what my mom said. My dad's claim to fame was chugalugging seven beers in a row. He probably died of alcohol poisoning before he was twenty-one." He stared at Syd with a challenge in his gaze. "My mom was fifteen when she found out she was having me. She managed to work at a coffee shop, take night school classes so she could get her high school diploma and raise me in between."

Syd wondered if Ki knew just how much of his love for his mother showed in his voice and facial expression. "I hope you remember her with a lovely Mother's Day card every May."

He grinned. "When I got my first advance check I told her I wanted to buy her a new Chevy. She said to make it a Buick instead. She figured one Chevy in her lifetime was enough!"

"Why aren't you spending Christmas with her?"

His features softened. "I don't think her husband would have approved of me going along on their honeymoon. They got married last fall and decided to wait until now to go on their honeymoon."

After Ki rinsed off the plates and placed them in the dishwasher, he paused and looked at Syd, who was busy playing with the dogs. "You don't intend to leave, do you?" He sounded more resigned to the fact than angry about it.

"No, I sure don't." She picked up Cocoa and combed his thick fur with her fingertips.

"And there's nothing I can say that might change your mind?"

"Not a thing."

Ki's shoulders lifted and fell with a deep sigh of resignation. "If the kids fool around with my laptop, I will not hesitate to do them bodily harm."

Syd thoughtfully held back her triumphant smirk. She always believed she was the better person if she acted the part of the gracious winner.

"I'll make sure they don't disturb you during your work," she replied.

Ki wanted to groan at the thought of the book. He came here because nothing was working right. He came here because he needed to be alone. When he began his book about Baskin he had no idea it would turn out to be one of the most difficult stories he'd ever tried to write. And now to top it off, he was going to have to put up with a red-haired witch and two waifs playing games with his mind. His apartment in Chicago was looking more appealing by the second. Until he looked at something else that was even more inviting.

"They might as well toss me in a padded room and throw away the key," he muttered, stomping out of the kitchen. "Next time I want peace and quiet, I'll try the North Pole."

"Wouldn't you like the last cup of coffee?" Syd called after him with studied solicitousness. All she received for her trouble was an angry mumble. "Then if you don't mind, I'll take it and make up a fresh pot for you."

She hummed a military march as she left the kitchen with the dogs fast on her heels.

It wasn't until a moment later Ki realized the knots of tension that had been in his body for the past few months were starting to unwind. And he had a pretty good idea that Syd Taylor had something to do with it. Trouble was, he worried that only meant she was going to create other kinds of tension.

SYD THREW ON her black parka and went outside to her Jeep. She punched in the code to disarm the alarm, and after telling the kids to keep close to the house, warmed it up and drove it around to the rear of the cabin so she could unload the contents.

She leaned inside to push aside a couple of boxes. As she reached forward toward an inner corner, a voice came from behind.

"Need any help?"

She looked over her shoulder to see Ki standing in the kitchen doorway.

"No, thanks, there isn't anything heavy," she assured him, silently damning herself for not sensing his presence. What was there about the man that upset her internal radar?

He nodded and went back inside.

"Such a gentleman," she laughed to herself, reaching back to the corner and carefully peeling back a section of the carpet. The panel's tiny green blinking light looked like something out of a James Bond movie, but it assured her no one had found it. Syd punched the buttons below in what appeared to be a random sequence and waited to hear the tiny click before she lifted a lever. A section of the Jeep's floor slid to one side, revealing two powerful rifles and three handguns with ammunition secured next to them. Like the Boy Scouts, Syd always believed in being prepared. And the guns weren't something she could have left behind at the house or even in the small apartment she kept when she was in town. So when she left, she took them with her. She made sure everything was intact before quickly closing the panel.

"A woman can never have enough firepower," she murmured, pulling out a box filled with Heidi and Jamie's toys she had made sure to bring along. While she hated the idea of taking them from their home, she wanted to make sure they had some of their belongings with them. "Jamie, would you come help me with this, please?"

Within seconds he'd skidded to a stop by his aunt. "Isn't child labor illegal?"

"Of course it is, my little darling. I would never have you do anything that would smack of labor. So I don't want you to worry about your toys. They'll be safe locked in the Jeep." She started to take the box from him.

He moved them out of her way. "No, that's okay. I'll help. I just hope my Game Gear didn't freeze. We shoulda brought it in last night."

"As it doesn't breathe, I don't think we have anything to worry about," Syd said amiably, carrying Heidi's box of toys toward the back door. Jamie followed.

Syd carried one box upstairs and instructed Jamie to leave the other downstairs. She'd take care of it later. He didn't waste any time in racing outside before his aunt got any more ideas.

She unpacked their duffel bags and put clothing away, then put the kids' toys out where they could easily find them. The last thing she took care of was setting a studio portrait of Shane, Jenny, Heidi and

Jamie on the dresser. Tears filled her eyes as she brushed her fingers against her brother's image.

"You can't protect the whole world, Syd," Shane told her the day she informed him she had signed up with the agency. *"Why do something so dangerous? Why can't you marry Andrew and have kids?"*

"Because marrying Andrew won't make me happy," she had told him. *"Because I need more than playing the part of the wife of an up-and-coming state senator. I'm not made for that kind of life."*

"Great! One person can't save the world, Syd. I don't want to see you killed for your efforts!" he had raged at her.

"I guess we got it all wrong, big brother," she whispered to the image of her three-minutes-older sibling.

Syd gave each dog a rawhide chew toy, laughing as Bogie immediately trotted off with his prize searching for an appropriate hiding place. It was a well-known fact that the small dog preferred to hide his treats. The only problem was he generally forgot where he'd hidden them. They didn't show up until someone stumbled on them behind the couch or beneath chair cushions.

She spent the next hour exploring the upstairs rooms, making sure the locks were secured on the windows and on the French doors that opened onto the second-story deck. Outside, she saw a stairway leading downstairs to the rear deck and a hot tub covered with a tarp. She stood at the window for a moment, watching the kids building a snowman in the yard.

She thought of the books she'd stashed in her bag when they left Virginia. There were a large number of novels she had been intending to read and never seemed to have the time for. Inactivity was something Syd was used to even if she didn't like it. She'd staked out more than her share of arms and drug dealers during her years as an agent, and she was always able to find ways to occupy herself. But her adrenaline was always running then. She had to keep herself on her toes at all times. Anticipation pumped her up and gave her a high no drug in the world could duplicate. She felt a curious letdown and started to feel sorry for herself until she thought of the kids. No, they were more than worth her taking on a slower, and safer, pace of life.

She looked around for Ki but couldn't find him in the living room or kitchen. That was when she noticed the laptop computer was missing from the table. Now she had a pretty good idea where he was.

"It isn't right that you hide out in here when it's your house."

Ki looked up from the screen covered with words that didn't make any sense to find Syd standing in the doorway.

"I'm not hiding out." He shifted from his cross-legged position in the middle of the bed to stretching his legs out in front of him. He set his computer to one side. "I tend to do my best work in a hall closet."

"Liar."

He shrugged. "Every creative mind has its little eccentricities. Mine's space. The less the better. That way my attention can't stray as easily."

Syd didn't wait for an invitation to enter. She walked in and seemed to wander aimlessly, sliding her forefinger across the top of the dresser as if checking for dust, glancing out the window and flicking her eyes toward the closet, where the door was open several inches.

To a less-discerning eye, she would have appeared to be idly curious about his room. Ki was positive she could be blindfolded and still easily name every piece of clothing visible in the closet. He'd bet she knew, to the penny, how much loose change was lying on top of the dresser. Hell, she probably could tell what color underwear he wore. If he'd had any on, that is.

Syd folded her hands against her lower spine and rested against the dresser.

"I understand you're a writer. What kind of books do you write?"

Any writer's ego was pricked when they weren't recognized. Ki wasn't any different.

"You're not a reader?"

"I like a good horror novel now and then. Psychological thrillers, too."

"I write true-crime novels," he said tersely.

Her lips twitched. Now, why the hell did she find his statement amusing?

"Who have you written about?"

"I wrote Caroline Matthews's story." He named a woman who'd murdered her boss because he refused to give her a raise, then had gone on to kill everyone in her office because she believed they were part of a conspiracy to keep her from getting what was due her. "I've written about Justin Stanley."

"Wasn't he that hermit who lived in a cave high up in the Rockies? He was kidnapping teenage girls out of campsites to keep him company in his cave until he got tired of them. Did the police ever find all the bodies?"

He shook his head. "Not up in those mountains. Too many places for him to hide them."

"Do you prefer the more sensational crimes or the subtle ones?"

He marveled at the way she could stand there, not moving a muscle. "Is there such a thing as a subtle crime?"

A slight shrug of the shoulder pushed her sweater neckline down another inch.

"I always considered poison subtle," Syd commented. "If you know what you're doing you can make if difficult to trace. There are a lot of rare ones out there without antidotes."

Ki thought about the delicious breakfast he'd consumed. Then the second pot of coffee Syd had made. He thought of the second cup he'd just finished.

"You're good," he stated in an admiring tone. "Very good."

"I have to be," Syd said with no show of conceit.

"Why?"

Her turning to look out the window looked so natural Ki had trouble believing it was deliberate. Deep down, he knew it was.

"Those kids are going to turn into icicles," she mused as she walked to the door.

Ki watched her glide across the room. He decided no normal woman walked with such grace. But there was something there. Something about her he couldn't quite put his finger on.

"What's for lunch?" he called after her, purely for the sake of saying something.

"Whatever the kids and dogs will eat."

"What about what I'll eat?"

"Something tells me you'll eat anything that you haven't had to cook yourself." Her voice drifted back to him.

"Right about now, I could go for a pretty big helping of you," he muttered, picking his computer up and placing it on his lap, which suddenly seemed to have grown.

"Bogie, what have you got there? Isn't that Cocoa's?" He heard Syd's voice from the kitchen. A dog's whine answered her question. "All right, but if Cocoa goes after you for taking his toy, I won't intervene. Come on, let's get you into a puppy snowsuit, so we can go outside."

Ki couldn't resist peeking out the window. Syd had added a parka to her sweater and pulled on boots. Cocoa was chasing after Jamie, who was, in turn, chasing his sister, who squealed in mock horror.

"That kid's lungs are going to give out before the month is out," he muttered, then burst out laughing when he saw the tan dog next to Syd.

Dressed in what looked like a black sweatshirt and sweatpants with his slightly crooked tail stuck through a hole in the back, Bogie danced alongside his mistress. It wasn't until he turned that Ki could see the bright red writing on his chest. Life's Short, Bite Hard.

"I wonder if that pertains to you or your mistress?"

He had no idea how long he stood at the window, watching the three humans and two canines dodge one another in a game of tag.

He might be a guy used to being alone, and liking it that way, but suddenly he wished he was out there with them.

He returned to his computer even though he still wasn't sure what angle he was going to take with this latest case. Probably because he didn't care.

Ki later discovered that lunch consisted of grilled cheese sandwiches and cream of tomato soup. Not gourmet fare but fine with him. Especially when he discovered that Syd had sprinkled bacon bits in the cheese and added a dash of Worcestershire. After lunch, she persuaded Heidi to take a nap. Jamie, occupied with his favorite video game, was slumped on the couch. Ki decided it was a perfect time to work— and an even more perfect time to question Syd a little more.

IT HADN'T TAKEN SYD long to realize any kind of housework wasn't her favorite activity. She preferred paper plates over china, and if dishwashers hadn't been invented she knew she would have invented one out of sheer desperation.

After lunch and getting Heidi and Jamie settled down, she returned to the kitchen with the resigned expression of a woman doomed to her fate. Luckily, the radio in the kitchen yielded a golden oldies station to listen to while she cleaned counters and washed the pans. With her hips swinging to the throbbing beat of Creedence Clearwater Revival, she handled the clean-up with a minimum of fuss.

Until Ki made the big mistake of walking up behind her to tap her on the shoulder as she put silverware away.

Syd didn't stop to think. She operated on pure instinct to protect. She had programmed herself into a protective mode for so long, she momentarily forgot she didn't have to worry about the enemy. The kids always spoke to her first instead of unexpectedly walking up behind her.

She spun on her heel, the other leg slightly extended to sweep her enemy off his feet. Before he'd hit the floor she had planted that same foot squarely in his solar plexus.

Air was pushed out of Ki's abdomen, leaving him gasping for oxygen. From his sprawled position on the floor, he stared up at her with disbelief in his eyes. She had taken him down so neatly. He coughed several times as he tried to take in enough air to speak. He finally managed to rasp out a few words.

"What the hell are you?"

Chapter Four

"Isn't that just like a man! A woman takes a *few* self-defense courses, so she can protect herself. Then the first time she has to use her skills, he gets all bent out of shape and automatically labels her another Bruce Lee." Syd silently congratulated herself on sounding properly affronted as she threw her hands up in an excellent portrayal of disgust.

"Bruce Lee's dead and that was no amateur throw you tried on me, honey. And don't talk to me about being bent out of shape." Ki slowly rose to his feet. He groaned as an aching pain shot up his back. "Damn, that hurt! You could have killed me!"

"Please watch your language," she requested sweetly. "There are children present. For someone who thinks he's dying, you seem to move around pretty easily."

"At least he says them in a language we can understand," Jamie spoke up. Both children stood in the doorway. Heidi yawned and rubbed her eyes.

"Why don't you kids go upstairs?" Ki suggested.

Jamie grabbed Heidi's hand and hauled her up the stairs. "Come on, they're gonna fight and they don't want us to hear them."

"We are not going to fight," Syd called after him.

"We are going to fight," Ki insisted between clenched teeth once he felt the kids were out of earshot.

Syd tipped her head back so that she could look fully into his face. The faint lines radiating from his eyes were tight with fury, as was his mouth. His eyes blazed with the brilliancy of strong lights hitting the facets of an emerald. His anger seemed to ooze out of his very pores.

"Aren't you afraid of high blood pressure?"

"Don't mess with me," he said quietly, dangerously.

"No problem." Little did he know she had faced greater dangers in her line of work. She considered him nothing more than a pesky mosquito.

Ki advanced on her until he stood close enough to see faint dots of light dancing in her eyes. "Sweetheart—" his endearment was thickly coated with sarcasm "—I've interviewed some of the most talented liars in the country. While you're very good at evading the truth, I know I can still catch you in a lie. Now, who are you?"

Not by a blink of the eye did Syd show any fear at his implied threat. She returned his gaze with a calm one of her own.

"Sydney Ann Taylor of Fairfax, Virginia. Would you like to see my driver's license for confirmation?

Although I understand fake driver's licenses aren't all that difficult to obtain if you know the right people.''

He didn't react to her less-than-subtle taunt. ''Is that your real name?''

Syd stood utterly relaxed. ''You know, I always thought a real name was an original name. But then I also thought my name would go better with an upper-crust British accent,'' she said, adopting the slight nasal tones of Great Britain's royalty. ''Don't you think it would add something?''

Ki took that extra step that had his chest brushing her breasts. He ignored the tingle entering his body. But he didn't ignore the faint narrowing of her eyes that had to mean she felt the same thing.

Interesting, he thought, tempted to go that extra inch to see what would happen.

He really needs to learn not to telegraph his moves, she noted to herself.

It was that mental pat on the back that momentarily drew Syd's attention from what happened next. Before she could regain her grasp on what was going on between them, Ki had grasped her forearms and pulled her toward him for that extra inch.

Her breasts met a hard chest covered in flannel. She noticed her nipples first tingled then hardened at the contact. That was her first mistake. Her second was opening her mouth to say something, because Ki wasn't about to give her a chance. He angled his hips against hers, and slid his hands down her spine until they rested in the hollow of her back, then moved one around to the front of her waist.

He discovered she tasted the way she smelled. Hot, silky, with a touch of exotic spice thrown in. It was a potent aphrodisiac to a man who couldn't remember any woman ever getting him so hot so fast. He curled his tongue around hers to further savor her taste, delighted when hers returned the favor.

Syd never thought a person's head could spin until now. She felt as if she was riding a swiftly revolving carousel that refused to stop. The world was whirling around her, and the only stable thing in her universe was the man holding her in his arms. A warm musky scent invaded her nostrils, wrapping her in a blanket of need. The scent of a man in heat, her disordered brain babbled. A scent that seemed to swirl around her and blend with her own. A perfect match. A dangerous match.

She wanted to pull away from him. She wanted to regain her senses, but she couldn't. And, if truth be told, the last thing she wanted to do was stop the earthquake starting to roll throughout her body.

If Ki ever wanted to know what heaven on earth was like, he now knew. It was Syd in his arms, kissing him back. Her arms were wrapped around him. Her breast was warm and swollen in his palm, her nipple a puckered rose.

He wanted more. He wanted them to find a nice quiet place and continue this in a horizontal position. He wanted her naked. He wanted—

"Wow, that is really gross!"

Syd and Ki flew apart. Syd's face was flushed, her eyes dazed as she tried to regain her self-control. Ki's chest was rising up and down rapidly as he sucked in much-needed air.

"Shouldn't you be upstairs, Jamie?" Syd asked with remarkable composure. She decided Ki ranked right up there with the top three kissers, and that included Sergei. She always thought he kissed better than he made love—and she considered him an incredible lover.

"You two were yelling."

She didn't take her eyes off Ki as she answered her nephew's argument. "We weren't yelling."

"You don't have to yell to sound like you're yelling." He made a face. "You guys were disgusting. I'm just glad Heidi didn't see you. She could have ended up with a complex." He turned around and trudged back up the stairs.

"You're welcome," Ki said.

She arched an arrogant eyebrow. "I don't believe I have a reason to thank you for anything."

He had the audacity to flash her a grin that was a perfect match for her arrogance. "Sure you do. Jamie was so disgusted with what he just saw he probably won't want to play doctor with the neighbor's daughter out behind the bushes for a long time. It's one less thing to worry about. My mom would agree since playing doctor used to be one of my favorite pastimes."

She shot him a "you've got to be kidding" look. "It's been a long time since you were nine, hasn't it?"

"It's been over twenty years, but boys don't change." He looked at her face—lean cheeks flushed a deep peach-rose color and lips moist and swollen—

and found he wanted her in just about every way imaginable.

Her eyes drifted downward for a second, then resolutely fastened on his face. "I've heard that a cold shower works wonders with problems like yours," she said with a sly twist of the lips. "Unless, of course, you'd prefer to *handle* it yourself."

Syd knew there were always times when it was smarter to retreat—and this was definitely a time to make a quick escape!

"I better check on Jamie and make sure he wasn't traumatized," she declared in a bright voice. She turned on her heel and walked up the stairs.

"Traumatized?" Ki muttered, stung by her remark. "Hell, he ought to consider it a damn good lesson," he muttered. As he walked back to his room, he realized just how hard he'd hit the floor. "I hate to think what she would have done to me if I'd fought back."

He settled down with his laptop in place. "Damn woman. She's probably the top finalist for Shrew of the Year award."

Syd walked quietly down the hallway until she stood just outside the room Jamie and Heidi were playing in.

"I don't like that man," she heard Heidi say. "He yells a lot."

"I think he likes to yell. Especially at kids," Jamie muttered.

"Why? We're not bad. I didn't wet the bed last night. And I picked up my clothes and put my toys away today."

Syd swore under her breath as she imagined tears sparkling in Heidi's eyes. She'd had an idea Jamie hadn't been pleased to see Ki kissing her. His tone confirmed it. She deliberately made noise before entering the room.

"All right, crew, we have a few hours free before dinner. Any suggestions?" she asked in a falsely cheerful voice as she stepped inside the room.

Jamie looked up with suspicion darkening his eyes. "Aren't you already busy?"

Syd dropped onto Jamie's bed. She ignored the large lumps decorating the badly made bed. She was just grateful Jamie had made it without any prompting from her.

"Do I look busy?"

"You did before."

"James Taylor, you are as blunt as your dad was," she pronounced.

Heidi looked up with eyes filled with tears and her tiny chin trembling. "I wanna go home."

Syd held out her arms and gathered her onto her lap. "I know, sweetie," she murmured, dropping a kiss on her forehead. "But we can't go back right now."

"'Cause Mean Mr. Leo doesn't want you to leave the agency?" She curled her arms around Syd's neck and nestled her damp cheek against her collarbone. "Jamie and me won't let him hurt you, Auntie Syd," she insisted. "Jamie can use his water pistol real good and I'll...I'll..." It was clear she wasn't sure what she was going to do. "I'll do something real bad to Mean Mr. Leo."

"Thank you, darling," Syd replied with equal ceremony, thinking of tiny Heidi going up against the cigar-chewing Leo. Now, that would be a show to watch. "I know the two of you will protect me and I love you for it."

"You could teach us how to throw people the way you threw Mr. Jones," Jamie suggested with just a touch too much eagerness.

She inclined her head. "I will show the two of you how to protect yourselves," she agreed, privately thinking of her peace-loving twin's horrified reaction to his children learning all about choke holds and knees in the groin. She wouldn't be surprised if her brother's ghost paid her a visit that very night. "But for now, what do you say we go for a drive?"

"Will it be safe? Mr. Leo won't be looking for you right away?"

From the time he began to speak, Syd had privately dubbed Jamie "the worrier."

"Since he knows how I feel about snow and cold weather, I doubt he'll think of me being out here."

"'Cause he knows you don't like it," Jamie clarified.

"It's not that I don't like snow. I *hate* it!" She laughed, catching him around the waist and pulling him on top of his sister. The tickling match was fast and furious with Jamie squealing and vainly trying to tickle Syd in return while Heidi launched herself into the battle.

The squeals and laughter filtered downstairs to Ki as he stared at the blank screen with the blinking cursor demanding its share of attention. He looked at the papers and photographs scattered around him. All part and parcel of the Baskin case he was slated to write about. For the moment, he couldn't think of a single word.

"I'm taking the kids out for the afternoon."

Syd's announcement swept through him like a frigid blast of air. He looked up.

She stood in the doorway, dressed warmly in the cream-colored sweater, jeans and boots. Her hair was tucked up under the navy knit cap. He couldn't put his finger on it, but there was something different about her. It was as if he wasn't looking at the same person.

"Is there anything you'd like me to pick up while we're out?" she asked politely.

"Who are you hiding out from?" he asked, without even being aware of the question forming in his mind.

"I ask you if you want anything and you ask me who we're hiding out from. Brilliant deduction. One goes with the other so well. Is that how you write your books? Jump from one insane subject to another? It must make it very difficult to link things together."

"Only a lawyer answers a question with another question. Except, honey, you don't look like a lawyer."

Syd thought of the law degree she had started out to attain, only to drop out to enter another area of the law.

"Why? Because I keep my distemper shots up to date? Or because I don't look like your typical vampire?" She playfully bared her teeth at him. "That's what I like about you, Jones. You take the bull by the horns. We'll get into this later. I promised the kids an afternoon out."

"Syd, if you're leery about taking your truck, you can take mine," he said suddenly, again speaking before he even thought about it.

She looked over her shoulder. "That's a very nice gesture, Jones. Thank you."

Ki listened to the kids' chatter as the threesome left the house. He jumped up and ran out into the living room just in time to see the Jeep roar down the driveway. Just in time to notice the vehicle sported a Nevada license plate although she had said she was from Virginia.

"Interesting," he murmured to himself.

A faint whimpering sound caught his attention. He looked down to find Bogie sitting up on his hind legs with a pleading expression in his eyes and Cocoa standing beside him.

"Potty detail, huh?" Both dogs' ears pricked up at the word. "Okay, why not? At least you can't talk my ear off." He opened the front door and gestured them outside.

As Ki watched the two dogs run for trees and bushes, it finally hit him why Syd had seemed like someone else. Her body language spoke to him differently. Her clothing seemed to hang on her body differently, making her look heavier than she really was. While her hair was tucked up under the cap, a wisp of dark brown bangs covered her forehead. And her speech pattern held a slight Eastern seaboard accent that hadn't been there before. He shook his head as he tried to figure out the puzzle.

"Maybe I'd better find out when "America's Most Wanted" is on TV. For all I know, she could be their lead story."

"Do we really have to stay back there?" Jamie asked Syd after she stopped at a drugstore to pick up childrens' aspirin.

She was learning the hard way to be prepared for anything where children were concerned.

Syd didn't start up the truck right away. She draped her arms over the steering wheel and turned her head to face him. "Yes, Jamie, we do."

"Why does Mean Mr. Leo want to hurt you?"

"He doesn't want to hurt me. He just doesn't understand that I want to quit my job."

"Dad said you can't quit the kind of job you have," he said quietly. "And if you didn't think Mr. Leo would hurt you, why do you always look different when we go out?"

Syd turned long enough to look in her rearview mirror. She wrinkled her nose at the dark bangs and darker-toned makeup that not only didn't suit her but did horrible things to her skin. She silently vowed she'd throw out her handy-dandy disguise kit for spies the day Leo finally admitted she was an ex-agent.

"It makes life more interesting." She gave her bangs a fluff and started up the Jeep. "Shall we try that playland that was advertised back there?"

"Yes!" Heidi bounced up and down in her excitement.

"Only if I don't have to play with her," Jamie muttered. But he couldn't hide his eagerness at going to the indoor playground.

"I don't want you to play with me," Heidi insisted.

"If you fight we don't go anywhere." Syd mentally patted herself on the back for sounding just like a mom.

She pulled in front of a large building advertising it held Kiddie's Ville, an enclosed playland boasting every kind of play equipment for all ages.

Syd ignored requests for candy as she paid a small fee for the kids to bounce on what looked like air-filled mattresses, climb a wide net to a playhouse and enter another room filled with various games and rides for small children.

She looked at the wall of pay phones, itching to call a few friends to find out if they knew anything about Leo's plans. But she wouldn't be surprised if he had their phones tapped.

"Why he has to be so pigheaded about my wanting to quit is more than any one person can understand," she murmured to herself, laughing as Jamie got tangled up in the net and then fought to get loose.

Even several hours later, Syd had trouble coaxing the kids to leave.

"Aren't you hungry?"

"Pizza!" Heidi shouted.

"No, we're going back to the cabin and have a nice dinner there," she said as she ushered them outside.

There was no missing their groans of dismay.

"What if we watch a videotape after dinner?" Syd was not beyond bribery.

"Homeward Bound?"

"Snow White."

Syd would have preferred something with more action, but she doubted Shane and Jenny would approve of her film choices. "Either one sounds good."

"What if *he* won't let us watch anything?" Jamie said flatly.

"Resist those two angelic faces? No one in their right mind could do that."

"Who says he's in his right mind?" Jamie countered.

Syd shot him a droll look. "Jamie, there are days when I really wonder about you."

"Yeah, Dad used to say that, too."

KI ALTERNATELY SWORE and mumbled to himself as he shuffled through papers and photographs in order to find one particular piece of paper.

"What'd you do with it?" he demanded of the two dogs who had followed him into the family room where he had sorted his research material into various piles on the coffee table. Cocoa had immediately plopped himself on the floor by the couch, where Ki had to step over him every time he needed to get up, and Bogie found his niche on the couch stretched out alongside Ki's leg. Neither dog stirred at his question. "I know they're here," he mumbled around the pen stuck between his teeth, rifling through another stack of photographs. "Finally!" He held up the object of his search.

He knew his quiet afternoon was over when the dogs ran for the front door barking and jumping up.

"We're back!" Syd sang out as the door opened and the kids ran inside.

"Lucky me."

She merely smiled at his sarcasm.

"Did you miss us?" she cooed.

"How could I miss you? You left your zoo behind."

"Unfortunately, I can't pass these guys off as kids wearing fur coats, although I've been tempted to try. They're better behaved than a lot of kids I've seen." Syd pulled off her knit cap and shook her hair free. She deftly unclipped the false bangs from the cap and tucked them into her coat pocket.

"Did you manage to escape from whoever you were supposed to?" Ki asked, tracking her movements.

"Aunt Syd said Mean Mr. Leo will never find us here because he knows she hates snow," Heidi piped up. As she realized what she'd just said, she clapped her hands over her mouth. "I'm sorry." The words were muffled by her covering hands.

"That's all right, sweetie," Syd assured her, giving her a hug.

"Mean Mr. Leo?" Ki echoed.

"A boss who refuses to admit his employees are allowed to quit," she said crisply, shooting him a look that demanded no more questions.

"We went to a special playland that had neat stuff to play on," Heidi told Ki. "And Jamie got stuck on a net!" She giggled.

He smiled at the little girl. "Sounds like you had fun. What about your Auntie Syd? What did she do?"

"She laughed."

Ki swung around when he saw movement out of the corner of his eye. He stiffened when he found Syd picking through the stack of crime scene and autopsy photographs he had been perusing.

He should have known there would be no horrified look of shock on her face when she leafed through photographs depicting a sick, violent mind. He was already realizing nothing could shock someone like Syd Taylor.

Syd handed them to Ki. "I always felt photos lacked the quality of really showing what happened at a crime scene." She headed for the stairs with the two dogs on her heels. "I would appreciate it if you'd keep them away from the kids. I'd like them to enjoy childhood as long as possible before they have to face the stark, cruel world."

There's only one answer, Ki thought as he dropped the photos in a manila enveloped and sealed it. *She's not real.*

Chapter Five

Ki was convinced he was well on his way on the road to insanity. He knew it wouldn't be long before the men in the white coats would come and take him away.

"Three days," he muttered between clenched teeth as he stabbed each key on the laptop's keyboard with his fingertips. "Three days of her Mrs. Rogers goodwill and smiles. Three days of dogs who come to me as often as they go to her to be put out. One goes out and the other doesn't want to. Five minutes later, the other one insists on going out." He spiked the *E* key again. "Then she bops around the place in those figure-hugging clothes of hers while the kids either act scared to death of me or look at me as if they hate me. And people wonder why I don't get married? Why should I when I have the perfect reason not to, right out there!"

"Excuse me?" Syd stood in the doorway with a plate in one hand and a cup in the other. "I thought you might like some fresh-baked cookies and coffee." She carried them inside and set them on the table by his elbow.

Ki stared at the plate. *She bakes?*

"Thanks."

Syd smiled, unaffected by his curt manner. "I'll leave you alone now."

"Good."

Ki waited until Syd was gone before he picked up one of the cookies and found it still warm. He bit into it and chewed.

"She bakes."

"Auntie Syd, are you going to bake all the refrigerator cookies you got at the store?" he heard Jamie asking. "Can I have some of the dough before you cook it?"

"Jamie!" Syd's whispered warning came a little too late. Ki grinned.

"Don't worry, Jamie," he said to himself. "It will be our little secret." He picked up the second cookie and happily munched away. "I wonder if this means most of our meals come out of frozen foods packages."

He returned to his story with more enthusiasm than he'd had in the past couple of days. If he wasn't careful, Thomas Baskin was going to come off a lot more sympathetic than the man deserved.

WHEN KI EMERGED from his bedroom hours later, he felt drained and positive his brain had melted away. As he went into the kitchen for a cup of coffee, he looked up, listening to Syd's soft tones overhead and faint thumping sounds as she talked to one of the children upstairs. But it was another soft voice in the next room that caught his attention.

"You be very careful driving to work." Heidi's childish voice reached him from a room off to the side of the living room. "Okay, bye."

Ki followed her voice and came upon a scene he considered to be the worst horror a man could discover in his own house.

His breath slammed out of his body as shock set in.

Agony sliced its hideous way through his veins.

He was positive he was dying.

He didn't want to believe what he was seeing. It was too horrible to contemplate.

Heidi had obviously taken one of the chairs and dragged it over so she could climb on top and sit down with all her Barbie and Ken dolls and all their paraphernalia. In her mind, she probably thought she had the perfect play area for her dolls.

In Ki's mind, Heidi had committed the worst crime known to man.

The little girl was sitting cross-legged on top of the pool table.

He opened his mouth and tried to say something, but nothing more than a tiny squeak could come out.

Heidi, smiling as she talked to her dolls, looked up. Instead of looking frightened at Ki's red face, she merely smiled.

"See, I'm staying out of your way," she informed him. "Just like Auntie Syd said I should."

"Yes." The word came out as a breath of air.

Ki's fists hung at his side. He didn't blame Heidi. She was a small child. No, he'd go after the person who deserved all the blame. As he took jerky steps toward the stairs he thought of Steve and Tripp extol-

ling the joys of matrimony. No way! Matrimony
meant kids. Kids meant you had to worry about them
playing with their dolls on your pool table. No thanks!
He'd prefer to deal with cold-blooded killers any day!

"Syd." He coughed as her name came out sounding strangled. "Syd!"

"What'd we do now?" He heard Jamie's plaintive
voice from above. "Breathe too loud?"

"Don't be sarcastic, dear," Syd chided. "That's my
department."

Ki was now growing furious. "Syd!"

He regretted calling her the moment she ran downstairs.

He had no idea what she had been doing upstairs,
but it had left a sheen of sweat on her face and throat.
Dressed in blue and rose print bicycle shorts and a
cream, rose and blue print T-shirt, she evidently had
been in the midst of some sort of exercise routine. Her
ponytail sagged to one side, wisps of hair stuck to her
moist cheeks, and her face wasn't entirely bare of
makeup. As she came closer to him, he realized wildly
that sweat on a woman could be erotic.

Maybe he broke up with that stockbroker too soon.

"Is there a problem?" Her drawl was a shade too
challenging.

"Yes, there is a damn problem," he muttered,
grabbing her arm and pulling her off to one side. "Do
you know where your niece is?"

Syd's eyes widened with a hint of fear. "She
wouldn't leave the house. She knows she isn't supposed to."

Ki had to tighten his hold to keep her from bolting. He felt guilty that he hadn't taken another tack.

"Syd, calm down. I didn't mean to frighten you. It's just that she's..." He took a deep breath as shock mingled with anger again roiled upward. "She's..." In the end, he slid his hand down to hers, laced his fingers through hers and pulled her out of the small hallway and into the other room. He settled for gesturing toward Heidi, who was again immersed in her play.

Syd caught herself just in time from asking Ki what the problem was.

Men and their toys, she thought to herself as she realized just what her niece had chosen for her playground. "Heidi, sweetheart, what made you choose the pool table to play on?"

Heidi's blue eyes, so much like her aunt's, lit up with joy. "Because it holds my Barbie Dream House and my Barbie swimming pool just right and I'm out of everybody's way."

Syd heard Ki's whimper of distress.

"She knows she's not supposed to put any water in the pool unless she has it outside," she whispered, keeping her smile firmly pasted on her face. "How did you get up there?"

Heidi pointed at the chair standing by the table. "I climbed up real careful. You don't want me playing on the floor 'cause it's too cold and I saw this and knew it would be perfect." She looked pleased with her choice of a play area.

"Get her off," Ki said in a faint voice.

"Honey, Jamie and I are practicing tuck and rolls. Do you want to come up and practice with us?" Syd walked over to the table and casually looked down into the swimming pool. She breathed a sigh of relief to see Heidi had remembered her instructions and hadn't filled it with water.

Heidi cocked her head to one side. Clearly, playing Barbie was waging a war with the idea of rolling around.

"Okay." She started to stand up.

"No!" Ki shouted at the same time Syd curved an arm around the little girl's rear end and picked her up. She set her on the floor and touched her fingers to her chin to lift it up.

"This table is very special and you probably shouldn't play on it," she told her. "We'll find you a better place for Barbie, okay?"

"But it holds everything up there."

"I know, but we'll still find somewhere else. Now, go upstairs and work out with Jamie. I'll pick up your toys for you."

Heidi shot Ki a broad smile as she hopped up the stairs.

"I'm sorry." Syd tossed Barbie and Ken into the pool and lifted it off while snagging the house with her other hand. "You have to remember she's a little girl and doesn't understand the significance of not violating a pool table with Barbie."

"I didn't yell at her. Don't I deserve something for that?"

She set everything down on the floor and started back toward the stairs.

"Probably."

Ki grasped her arm and pulled her back around to face him. He suddenly pulled off the elasticized band holding her ponytail. With it loosened, her hair tumbled down around her face. As he touched her skin he found it warm and damp against his fingertips.

He suddenly wanted to find out if she felt that way all over. If she felt that way when she made love. Did she put all her energy into it, as she did everything else? Awareness of her sprang up. As did other parts of his body.

"Let go of me," she whispered, remaining very still in his hold. She knew it wouldn't have taken any strength to free herself, but she couldn't find it in her to do so.

Ki's nostrils flared as the warm, womanly scent of her skin, coupled with the salty tang of her perspiration, drifted upward. What would it take just to bury himself in that erotic fragrance?

"You were the one who wanted to stay." He moved closer until his chest brushed against her breasts.

"Auntie Syd!"

Ki didn't imagine the faint regret in her eyes as they heard Jamie's shout.

Syd took her time stepping back. "I'm being paged." She started up the stairs.

"You know the nice thing about kids?" Ki asked her when she reached the halfway point up the stairs.

"That they're smaller than you?" She continued her ascent. "And that they pretty much believe anything you tell them?"

"No matter what, they have to go to bed."

Syd's foot faltered on the last step as his words registered. After that little slip in her composure, Ki had to admire her control as she looked over her shoulder.

"Yes, but I wonder who will worry about whom when that time comes?"

With that she continued walking with her gliding step toward the rear of the cabin.

Ki whistled softly under his breath as he returned to his writing. She had an amazing way of increasing his creative juices.

"I CAN'T BELIEVE IT. You have tapes for every episode." Syd rummaged through the cabinet of videotapes. "You even have the original pilot. This is fantastic." She pulled out a tape at random and read the description.

"My idea of relaxation is a "Star Trek" marathon." Ki was content to sit in the large chair with his legs propped up on the matching ottoman and admire the view. As a man who usually chose a woman a little more on the voluptuous side, he was finding Syd's lean figure a joy to watch. Especially since her choice of clothing defined every curve and angle, although he doubted she chose it with that in mind. With what he had discovered about her so far, Syd dressed for comfort, not for looks. She wore brown leggings with heavy brown socks covering her feet and a rust-colored wool top that highlighted the brilliant hair she had brushed away from her face. "Go ahead. Choose a few."

Her face lit up. "I only got hooked on the new show several months ago when I first saw the program. I've had to settle for the episodes in syndication so I could catch up."

Ki frowned. "How could you miss something that's found everywhere?"

Syd thought of the places she'd spent time in where a television set wasn't necessarily a part of a household.

"It happens sometimes." She pulled out several more cassettes before she made her choice.

Ki leaned down to pick up the bottle of beer he'd kept by the chair. "Syd, I'm a writer. I tend to dig for the truth. And honey, so far all you've told me is crap. I just may have to do a little digging about you."

She stood up and walked over to the VCR, inserting a cassette. She waited until the images flickered on the television screen before sitting on the floor near Ki's chair. She curled her legs to one side, cradling a large bowl of popcorn in her lap. She wasn't the least bit upset about the idea of his digging around for information about her. Not when she knew that was completely impossible.

"Jamie's going to be real upset if he wakes up and finds us down here watching 'Star Trek: The Next Generation' and eating popcorn," she commented, tossing a couple of kernels into her mouth, then handing several pieces to each dog who watched her with pleading eyes.

"He's a kid who needs his sleep."

"That's not the way he looks at it."

"Why 'Next Generation' and not the original?" he asked when the credits rolled across the screen. "The original is much better."

"I watched the original when I was growing up, and I've decided I prefer Jean Luc and Riker to Kirk and Spock." She held the bowl up to him.

He scooped up a handful. "There's no comparison." He pointedly ignored Cocoa and Bogie when they turned their attention to him.

"That's right, there's no comparison. Jean Luc has class. Kirk doesn't." Syd smirked, setting the bowl back in her lap. "Now be quiet. I've never seen this episode."

Ki slumped down in the chair. He wasn't interested in the tape when watching Syd was much more intriguing. He braced his chin on his palm and studied her facial expressions as she became engrossed in the story. He wondered if she'd deck him if he suddenly pulled her into his lap. He wondered if watching Jean Luc and Riker would put her in a seductive mood.

"See what I mean," she said suddenly, pointing at the screen. "The two men are great together. It's almost a toss-up. Although there are times when I wouldn't mind seeing if I could fry Data's circuits." She wiggled back and forth.

Ki blinked. Watching her was proving to be a dangerous proposition.

Fry my circuits. Go ahead, fry mine.

He cleared his throat.

"Think you could pass the popcorn back here?"

Syd didn't turn around as she handed him the bowl over her shoulder. Ki took the bowl out of her hand

and scooped up another handful. He started to nudge her shoulder with the bowl, then changed his mind. He set the bowl on the floor next to his beer and concentrated on the program.

Without taking her eyes off the screen, Syd dipped her hand in her lap. She looked down when she found it empty.

She twisted at the waist. "Could I have the popcorn, please?"

He looked the picture of innocence. "What popcorn?"

"The popcorn bowl I handed you a few minutes ago," she said with great patience.

Ki held up his hands, wiggling his fingers. "Do I look as if I have any popcorn?"

"Very funny." She uncoiled her body and walked across the carpet on her knees. "Where did you put it?"

"I don't have it!" he argued, pretending to be hurt by her accusation.

"Don't argue with me about popcorn," Syd muttered, starting to look over Ki's sprawling body. She was so intent on looking for the bowl she didn't see his hand grab her wrist and unbalance her. Syd squealed as she fell on his body.

"Hey!"

Ki burst out laughing at the indignation etched on her face. And in her eyes. Those incredible blue eyes discharged blue sparks the same way the flames in the fireplace sparked.

"This is not funny."

"I think it is." He tried to stop, but once started, he found he couldn't. Every time he looked at her and noted the ire in her eyes he started chuckling again.

"It is not funny!" She pounded his chest with her fists.

He wrapped an arm around her waist, pulling her even closer as he tried to stop her attack.

"All this over some popcorn?"

"You better be glad it isn't chocolate, buster or you'd be black and blue by now! People have died for little more than picking up a piece of my chocolate." Syd realized her mistake the moment she stuck her face in his.

Green eyes darkened to a deep jade color. Blue eyes blazed with sapphire lights. Respiration increased. Awareness heightened between the two until it seemed to be a thick blanket surrounding them.

Syd looked at Ki as if she was trying to make up her mind. It didn't take her long to come to her decision.

The little witch, Ki thought when he watched the tip of Syd's tongue sweep across her bottom lip. *She's trying to seduce me.*

"What's the matter, Jones?" she whispered, toying with a button on his shirt as she deftly shifted her body around until she lay fully on top of him. "You need an engraved invitation?"

"I wanted to make sure you didn't try to hurt anything important if you thought I was getting out of hand," he said softly, lifting a strand of hair and watching it float back downward. "I've already learned it isn't safe to sneak up on you."

She smiled. "I like an honest man." With a flick of her finger, she loosened one button then the next until his shirt lay open on his chest. She eyed the expanse of crisp dark hair. "There's something very sexy about a man who has hair on his chest."

Ki hated to act suspicious or paranoid, but this wasn't what he'd come to think was Syd's usual behavior. He ignored the soft growling by his side and hoped the dog wouldn't decide to take a chunk out of him.

"Bogie, it's all right," Syd assured the dog without taking her eyes from Ki's face. "Go lie down."

"Sounds good to me."

Syd grinned. "I was talking to the dog."

Ki shifted to one side, groaning when Syd slid down against him. He turned onto his side facing her.

"Why?"

She didn't pretend not to understand the meaning of the question.

"You, me, popcorn, outer space. What more could a woman ask for?" Her smile gradually faded. "It's been a tough year. Maybe I'm just making sure I haven't turned into an ugly crone, and you seem to be eager to show me I haven't."

"No, you're not a crone." Ki used his fingertip to trace random circles on her cheek. "In a very short span of time, you've lost your brother and sister-in-law, left your job, and taken on the care of your niece and nephew. You've even gone so far as to move to the opposite end of the country because you feel the kids need a change. You're obviously not the mom type, but you're sure as hell trying. Tell me something, Syd.

With you concentrating so much on the kids to make sure they're happy, who takes care of you?''

Her facial muscles froze until they appeared to be carved from stone. Moisture shimmered in her eyes before she forced it away and her lips slightly tightened.

Ki never knew a person could have so much control over their emotions. If he hadn't seen that brief show, he would have thought she didn't have a soul. He had to admire her, but seeing that kind of control also had him wanting to see if he could make it crack. He wanted to push her the way he pushed one of his subjects.

He wanted to see the real Syd Taylor.

"Come on, Syd," he cajoled, running his hands along her sides. "What about those long nights when you're lying in bed by yourself? What do you think about? Some guy from your past?" He wished he hadn't asked that question since it was the last thing he wanted to know about. "Do you miss your old life? Do you wish you could make life go back to what it was? To that life Jamie and Heidi only hint about?"

"You don't know anything about my life," she said firmly, surprising him with her vehemence. "Yes, I want life to go back the way it was, because then my brother and sister-in-law would be alive again to cherish those two children they created. You didn't see the scum who killed them. Well, I did. I stood there and looked at him cowering in a corner of his jail cell because he knew if I had my way he would have died slowly and horribly by my hand." Her nails raked his chest, leaving welts. "And he knew I would have done it and no one would have stopped me. He's in prison for what he did and I only hope he's praying I won't find him again.''

Ki stared at Syd as if she was a total stranger.

''Are you ever going to tell me the truth, Syd? Are you ever going to trust me enough to tell me exactly who you are?''

Her shoulders rose and fell with the deep breath she took. Her hair parted from her nape, leaving the tender skin exposed as she stared at the seat cushion while she deliberated. She straightened up. She reached across Ki for the remote control and punched the mute button.

''Very few people know exactly what I do,'' she said finally, meeting his gaze with her own level one. ''Considering the nature of your work, I can either place my trust in you or I can lose a lot by not telling you.''

Ki cupped her cheek with his palm. He noticed how she tipped her head to one side, allowing her face to be cradled by his hand. He figured there was hope.

''I don't betray people's secrets, Syd,'' he said quietly.

Her chest rose and fell again in a resigned sigh.

''Syd, you're not on the run, are you? That's not the reason for the disguises and fake accents and everything?'' he asked. ''Because if you really are, I can help. I have contacts all over the country. Let me help you.''

She smiled sadly at his sincere offer. ''I'm on the run but not for the reason you think. I chose to go into hiding from my boss because he's being stubborn and refusing to accept my resignation. He figures he can get me to keep working for him. He's even gone so far as to offer to pay boarding school fees for the kids, and believe me, he doesn't part with money all that easily. So I'm hoping if I stay out of sight long enough he'll get the message and leave me alone.''

"No one has to hide from their boss unless they stole something he wants back." He narrowed his eyes.

"That proves you've never had the joy of meeting Leo, who looks more like a thirties theatrical agent than the director of a government agency." Syd looked off into the distance then back at Ki. "Let me put it this way. Agents aren't supposed to have a reason to resign. When they get too old to go out in the field they're supposed to man a desk or teach incoming recruits. While they don't come right out and say you can't quit outright, the International Security Agency does not accept resignations. And that is why we're hiding out.''

Ki stared at Syd. Once again, the lady had left him at a loss for words.

Chapter Six

Syd watched the varied emotions, ranging from astonishment to comprehension, play across Ki's face as he mulled over her revelation. She scooted backward until she could comfortably sit cross-legged on the ottoman. For the time being, she thought it prudent to keep some distance between them.

"What's wrong? Don't you believe a woman can be as good as James Bond?" She knew the only way she could finish what she'd begun was to continue on the offense. "Women can handle the fancy gadgets just as well as any man. We can shoot just as straight."

He shook his head. Whether it was because of her question or something going through his mind, she wasn't certain. He leaned back in the chair and put his clasped hands behind his head as he stared up at the ceiling. He knew he wouldn't find any answers there, but it was easier to look up there than to look at Syd's oh-so-serious face.

"I thought about our first meeting when I wasn't sure if you were going to pull a gun or a knife on me or just kill me with your bare hands, which I'm sure you can do." A slight nod of the head told him he was correct. "And then there was that time in the kitchen when I startled you. I should have realized that only someone well trained in self-defense could have thrown me so effortlessly." He tipped his head down to look at her. "You didn't react like most women would have when I came up behind you. They would have jumped and maybe screamed bloody murder for scaring them. Your answer was to almost punch my lights out. Okay, fine, you're a government employee. A civil servant, so to speak. What other surprises do you have in store for me?"

Syd's shoulders rose and fell in a resigned sigh. She decided it wouldn't be prudent to tell him just yet about her little stash of weapons hidden in the back of her Jeep. She didn't think he'd take the news very well.

"No gadgets. I told you before. I quit and Leo refuses to accept my resignation. And what he doesn't want, he doesn't allow," she said quietly. "He hates change with a passion. A field agent's resignation means he has to have another one trained and ready to go in. He doesn't like that. Not just because it's a lengthy process to slip a new person in. It can be a dangerous proposition. And I'm not bragging when I say I was very good at what I did."

She noticed the muscles along his jawline tense at her words.

"Wait a minute. Are you saying you were a field agent?"

She nodded.

Ki looked at her with narrowed eyes as he mulled it over. "Are we talking you traveled around the country looking for killers, or you traveled around the world looking for even worse scum?" he asked in a quiet, controlled voice.

Syd sensed she was facing a force much more dangerous than anything she'd faced before. Ki was proving to be more of a challenge than anyone she'd ever dealt with.

"Or can't you tell me because your assignments were confidential?" This time there was a decided bite to his question.

"Since you appear to have the contacts, why don't you find that out for yourself?" She retaliated with her only weapon: words. "After all, you did say something about checking me out."

"If I had any contacts with the ISA, I'd be on the phone with them right now to check this out." His eyes glittered with green lights that didn't look exactly friendly. Still, they ignited a pool of heat in the pit of her stomach.

"It's agency policy not to divulge the identity of their agents to anyone. Not even the president of the United States could call up and receive information. Leo prides himself on practicing paranoia to the extreme. Believe me, he can make the CIA sound like blabbermouths."

"Then you could tell me anything you'd want and I wouldn't be able to find out if you were telling me the truth, would I? If you're all so secretive, why did you tell me all this?"

She shrugged. "I don't see any reason to keep my occupation a secret any longer. Especially since I'm now out of the business. Besides, you might be a writer, but I still feel I can trust you.''

''What about the friend who got you the use of the cabin? Can you trust him, too?''

She nodded. ''I can trust him because he doesn't know everything about me.''

''Ex-lover?'' He didn't care if the question was too personal. He figured they were heading fast past that stage, anyway.

The smile on Syd's face held just a touch of the tease. ''Would it bother you if I said yes? Or if I said he wasn't an ex-lover *yet?*''

''Damn straight it would bother me!'' He straightened up, planting his feet on the floor as he leaned toward her. ''Sweetheart, if there's one thing I don't do, it's poach in another man's territory.''

She raised a delicately arched eyebrow. ''How noble of you.'' She wasn't sarcastic, merely observing.

''I'd just like to point out I'm not anyone's territory. And definitely not anyone's property. My love life has taken a back seat to those two kids upstairs. The last thing they need right now is men trooping in and out of their lives.''

Ki nodded approvingly. He remembered his growing up with various ''uncles'' inhabiting his mother's life and bed. He was always grateful to her for never neglecting him even when her love life turned tumultuous, but he hated most of the men who wooed her with sweet words and ignored him. He learned whose side his mother was on the time one of the men hit him. She booted the man out without a second thought. He knew if it hadn't been for her faith in him

and her pushing him into college, he wouldn't be
where he was. Or have the close friends he had valued
since college. He always felt it was Steve, Tripp and
Deke who helped ground him the times he needed it.
No matter who needed help, each knew the other three
were only a phone call away.

"Yeah, you seem to have done a great job in keeping those kids in one piece. But like I asked you before, what about when the nights are long and cold?
When the walls seem to grow a little too close, who
looks after you? Who helps you banish the demons?"

Her posture stiffened at his softly worded question.

"Do I look like someone who has to worry about
demons?"

"I think there's more to the story than you traveling more than three thousand miles to make the kids
happy. They say they were happy in their home."

"They wouldn't have been happy if Leo or his un-
derlings were camping on the front steps," she countered. "They would have been scared to death.
Unfortunately, thanks to the media, they learned how
their parents died. The press felt they had to know how
two children felt losing their parents like that. They
tried again after I came on the scene, but I took care
of that," she added grimly. There was no doubt her
way of taking care of it wouldn't have stopped at a few
broken bones to make her point. "Since then, they're
very uneasy if strangers come too close to them."

"Because they're afraid they could get hurt, too,"
he guessed.

She nodded. "I restricted their television viewing as much as I dared and I kept them busy with a lot of physical activities. I figured if they were tired out, they wouldn't think about it. And if they were tired, I usually was, too. That way, I couldn't think about it, either."

Ki looked at Syd with eyes soft with compassion. He leaned forward, grasped her arms and pulled her into his lap as he dropped back into the chair.

"Tell you what, Syd. Why don't you just relax and let me do the watching?" His voice was a soft rumble in her ear. "A few minutes wouldn't hurt."

She sat stiffly in his embrace, but Ki didn't allow her to fight him. Not even mentally. He ran his hand up and down her back in a slow, sweeping caress, meant to relax her. While the words he murmured in her ear didn't make any sense, they helped chip away at the resistance in her body.

It took a while, but eventually, Syd started to loosen the tight hold she held on herself. She slowly inclined her body against his chest, curled her legs around his thigh and nestled even closer. He gathered her against him and tucked her head under his chin.

"That wasn't so bad, was it?" he murmured, tucking a stray hair behind her ear. He inhaled the soft, exotic fragrance he now equated with her.

Syd felt more than a loosening in her muscles as Ki continued to pet her softly and whisper in her ear. For too long, she had been keeping her emotions in check, doing everything possible to keep the children's spirits up, keeping an eye out for Leo's men and trying to forget the insane life she had led for the past ten years.

"I became an agent because I wanted the excitement," she said softly. "Correction. I *needed* the excitement."

Ki gave an imperceptible nod. He was silently relieved she had offered even that little crumb of information. "Who were you trying to prove yourself to, Syd?"

She muttered every profanity she knew in every language in her memory banks.

"Very good," he complimented her, in awe of her mastery. He secretly vowed to learn some of what sounded like the more colorful profanities. "And now that you've gotten that out of your system, are you going to answer my question about your work?"

"Not if I can help it."

"Is it considered classified material?"

"It's just none of your business."

Ki grinned. He wondered if he would have to keep pushing Syd's buttons to get the answers he wanted.

"I will tell you this. I was a danger junkie. Bungee jumping, skydiving, rock climbing. You name it. I tried anything that got the adrenaline pumping."

"Hell, if you wanted to get yourself pumped up, a good bout of hot, raw sex would have accomplished the same thing," he said facetiously.

Syd tipped back her head with her eyebrow cocked. "Trust me. It isn't even close to being the same thing."

Usually Ki would eagerly pursue a line like that. This time, he thought it prudent not to. Instead, he slowly loosened his hold on Syd, in case she chose to move away. He felt an odd pang of sorrow when she did just that.

"I think it would be a good idea if I go upstairs now," she said quietly, slowly uncoiling her body from around his. She looked down and burst out laughing. "That will teach you to put the popcorn in puppy reach."

Ki followed her gaze and found Cocoa's and Bogie's faces buried in the popcorn bowl. Cocoa lifted his head, licking his chops and looking as if he was asking for more.

"Is there anything they don't eat?" he asked Syd.

"Popcorn has always been one of their favorites. Come on, little piglets. Time for you guys to escort me upstairs."

Ki wasn't about to let her get away with the last word. He stood up and blocked her escape by placing his hands on her shoulders.

"You having a problem, Jones?" Syd asked, looking up at him with the expression he was rapidly getting to know as a defiant one. He wondered how many men in the past had been intimidated by that look. He already knew he wasn't one of them.

Instead of answering, he lowered his head and dropped the lightest of kisses on her lips. He stepped back before she could retaliate.

"We'll have to try for the "Star Trek" marathon another night." He kept his smile and voice noncommittal. "Maybe a battle of the captains. Kirk versus Picard."

Syd was halfway up the stairs before her soft-voiced reply drifted down to him.

"No contest. Picard's intelligence always wins hands down."

Ki dropped back on the chair, unaware of the broad grin stretching his facial muscles.

"No contest here, either. The lady is hot for me."

SINCE THE MORNING was cold and crisp instead of freezing, Ki opted to take his coffee out onto the rear deck and enjoy the beginning of the day. He dropped a cushion onto one of the redwood chairs and settled in.

"Hey, boy, never thought you were so crazy you'd sit outside in the snow. December ain't like July up here, no sirree."

Ki narrowed his eyes against the morning sun and waited until a dark figure disengaged itself from the trees.

The man could have been fifty or eighty. White hair curled wildly around a leathery face that was partially hidden by an equally ragged beard. His parka was army issue, circa World War II. Ki guessed his weather-beaten fatigues and laced up leather boots came from the same era.

"Hi, Zeke, how ya doin'? Have a seat." He gestured to a nearby chair. "Want some coffee?"

"You got any bourbon?" Zeke walked up and slowly lowered himself into the chair, his joints creaking loudly in protest.

"Not at eight o'clock in the morning. Besides, all you do when you drink the good stuff is tell people your private stock is much better. Why should I give you the chance to insult my good bourbon?"

"Mine *is* better than all that fancy stuff." He looked off into the distance. "Heard you had a woman staying here. Thought you boys came up here to get away from women.''

Ki sipped his coffee. "A friend and her niece and nephew are visiting for a few days.''

The old man snorted. "Hell, I thought you'd got smart and brought a woman up here for some slap and tickle. You boys coming up here all these years and not doin' more than drinkin' and playin' pool and other stuff didn't seem right. I mean, a place way out here is what a man and woman want so they can have some privacy. To do what they're supposed to do. Ain't natural for you not to want that.''

"We like getting away where there aren't any women," Ki told him. "Up here, we can do all those guy things women don't like.''

"But you let that woman and her kids stay here?''

"Just as a favor.''

"You forgot to mention she's got damn annoying little dogs," Zeke muttered. He turned his head at the sound of barking. "Now, what kind of person has fur balls like that? She must be one of those little social-ites." Disdain was heavy in his voice.

Ki bit his lip to keep from laughing at Zeke's com-ment. He decided it would be more fun for Zeke to find out for himself. He looked over his shoulder to see Bogie standing on a table so he could look out the window. Right now, the small dog's body was quiv-ering as taut as a bowstring as he stared past the men at something in the trees. He looked as if he would crash through the window at any moment.

He groaned. "Aw, hell, Zeke, you didn't bring that ugly cat of yours with you, did you?''

"I don't tell Peterson where to go and he doesn't tell me where to go," Zeke pronounced.

Ki shook his head. "I can't imagine your commanding officer was so horrible that you had to name your cat after him."

"It wasn't so much he was a son of a bitch," Zeke replied. "It was because the cat walks like him."

"Ki, Auntie Syd said to—" Jamie skidded to a stop before Zeke. He looked at the old man with horror in his eyes.

"Jamie, this is Zeke," Ki said. "He lives over the next hill."

Jamie kept a respectful distance and didn't take his eyes off the man. "Is he why Bogie's barkin' and Cocoa's howlin'?"

Zeke cackled. "Son, that ain't real barkin' and howlin' they're doin'. They just want a piece of my cat, and let me tell you, he'd whip their ass in no time."

"Zeke, we're trying to keep it clean here," Ki remonstrated in a mild tone.

The older man shrugged. "The boy's got to learn the right words sometime. Don't let that woman coddle him. Won't help him when he gets older."

"Auntie Syd coddle anybody?" Jamie laughed then looked confused. "What does coddle mean?"

"Baby," Ki clarified.

"Auntie Syd doesn't baby anybody." He kept a cautious eye on Zeke as he spoke to Ki. "She said if you want breakfast you have to come in now or she'll feed yours to the dogs."

Ki heaved a sigh as he pushed himself out of the chair. "She will, too. Want to come in for some breakfast?"

Zeke shook his head. "I don't let any woman threaten me, and you shouldn't, either, son. 'Sides, you're one of those men who don't need a woman full-time. You better go in there and show her who's boss."

"Yeah, well, she has methods of making a guy behave that are downright scary. Bogie, knock it off!" he shouted to the small dog who was now throwing himself at the window in his eagerness to get to the cat. "That cat would chew you up and spit you out."

Zeke heaved himself out of his chair. "Come over some evenin' and we'll have a snort," he invited as he took his leave.

Ki shuddered at the thought of Zeke's rotgut. He hadn't forgotten the first time he and Tripp, Steve and Deke had spent an evening at Zeke's cabin and indulged in the older man's homemade brew. To this day, none of the men could remember what happened that night, how they got back to their cabin or how they were still alive the next morning.

"Yeah," he muttered. "Take it easy, Zeke."

"He's scary," Jamie muttered, watching the old man amble off into the trees.

"He's not so bad," Ki assured him. "It's just that he's lived up here for so long he's forgotten how to be sociable to anyone but that mangy cat of his."

Jamie cast Zeke's retreating figure a wary look as he headed for the door.

"I bet he's Mean Mr. Leo in disguise," he muttered, pulling the door open. "Ki's comin'!" he yelled at the top of his lungs.

"Thank you for the report, James." Syd stood at the table, forking waffles onto each plate. Heidi already sat at the table with an expectant look on her face as she eyed the waffle Syd had set in front of her. "Now, go wash your hands."

"Ki said the man's name was Zeke, but I bet he's really Mean Mr. Leo."

"Mean Mr. Leo prefers wing tips over combat boots," Syd said serenely. She nodded at Ki as he took his chair. "Heidi asked for waffles and since they're easy to make, her request was granted."

"They're the kind you put in the toaster," Heidi confided to Ki.

"I don't like people who give away my secrets." She cut Heidi's waffle into bite-size pieces and poured a bit of syrup over them. "I noticed there's a riding stable not far from here that's still open. I thought I'd take the kids. Would you like to take a break from your writing and go with us?"

"Horseback riding? In this weather? Do you realize how cold it is out there? Are you sure the kids should be out in it?"

Syd shrugged off his protest. Obviously the temperature was a low priority to her. "I'm not worried about them. These kids grew up in cold temperatures. Come on, it will be fun." She leaned across the table. "I'll help you with your book later."

Ki was instantly suspicious of her generous offer. "How can you help me?"

He decided she had the kind of smile that should be angelic but had more than a hint of the devil. "I'll read all those police reports you have and explain them to you in layman's terms."

"I've been writing true-crime books for about eight years now," he said evenly. "I think I can figure out the meaning of all those big nasty words cops use."

"What about the feds' reports?"

"Confusing, but I've always liked puzzles." Ki put down his fork. "In case you don't get my meaning, I prefer to work alone."

"Maybe so, but I bet it isn't as much fun." Syd bestowed a bright smile on him. "I thought we could leave about ten. Is that all right with you?"

Ki searched his mind for a memory of his agreeing to go along. At best, he considered horses an unnecessary evil. There were a lot of other things he'd prefer to do. Trouble was, they wouldn't have included the kids.

"You're goin' to go, aren't you?" Jamie asked. "I don't want to be the only boy. It's bad enough goin' with Heidi, though Auntie Syd is really fun 'cause she doesn't act like a grown-up."

He knew he couldn't say no now. It wasn't Jamie's comment about Syd, but the hopeful look in the little boy's eyes that touched him. He should have realized that Jamie hadn't been hanging around him some days just because he was bored. He hung around because he missed his father and Ki was obviously the closest thing to a father figure he could find. Ki felt sorry the boy had to settle for him.

"Thanks, Jamie!" Syd looked affronted. "I'm about the best grown-up a kid could have and you know it."

Ki had a sinking feeling he wouldn't be walking too well that evening. "That does it. I'm going. You definitely need an adult along for this field trip."

"YOU OKAY, JAMIE?" Syd looked over her shoulder.

Jamie had been given a pony who plodded along behind the pinto Syd rode. Heidi rode happily sitting in front of Syd. At first, she'd passionately argued that she wanted a horse like Jamie, until she realized riding with Syd meant she was on a bigger horse than her older brother. Ki brought up the rear riding a docile bay.

"Make him go fast, Auntie Syd," Heidi ordered, bouncing up and down in her aunt's embrace.

"Heidi, we'll look for a merry-go-round for your fast horse," Syd told her. "We're just going to walk our horses through the woods and enjoy the scenery."

"And freeze our asses off," Ki muttered, pushing his chin into the collar of his parka. Still, he had to admit that watching Syd, resplendent in her black parka and black jeans, was worth being in the cold. A black felt gambler's hat with a red snakeskin hatband sat boldly on her head, while her hair was pulled back in a French braid.

She looked over her shoulder. "Are you all right?" Her bright blue eyes twinkled merrily as if she guessed he was cold and already a bit sore and more than a little horny watching her move smoothly in the saddle.

He put on his macho male act. "Never better."

Syd flashed him a smile that told him she knew he was lying.

"I wanna go fast!" Heidi shrieked, bouncing up and down. "Why can't we go faster?"

"Knock it off, Heidi!" Jamie ordered. "You're scarin' my horse."

"You're not on a horse, you're on a pony!" she taunted. "Baby on a pony! Baby on a pony!"

"Enough!" Ki's order snapped out like a bull-whip.

"But horses are supposed to go fast, not walk!" Heidi argued.

"Out here in the snow, it's better they walk," Ki told her. "If they run in the snow they could hurt themselves."

Heidi's lower lip pushed out as far as it could go. "Not fair."

"That's life," he said cavalierly.

"Good reason," Syd muttered, keeping a tight hold on the little girl who was still so excited she couldn't sit still.

As they rode along the trail, Ki thought back to all of them climbing into Syd's Jeep. And the way the rear of the truck looked a little different, although he couldn't quite put his finger on the difference.

"What do you carry in the back of that heavy-duty machine of yours, Syd?" he asked. "Come on, we're out in the open where there's no one around who can hear you. And you know you can tell me."

"You mean my spare tire, roadside emergency kit and a couple of blankets?"

"Auntie Syd, I wanna go fast!"

"*Stop it!*" Jamie shouted, glaring at his sister. "Heidi, you know you can't go fast, so stop asking!"

"I can if I want to!" Heidi almost leaped out of Syd's grip as she reached for her brother.

Syd had to do some quick maneuvering to keep Heidi in the saddle and her mount under control. Jamie's grip on his reins loosened a little and the pony spooked. As the pony wheeled in a tight circle, Ki reached out to grab the reins and regain control.

Ki had no idea how it happened. All he knew was that he somehow lost his grip on his own reins. Before he knew it, he had slid out of the saddle, banging his shoulder against a rock. Pain exploded in his shoulder and head at the same time.

"Auntie Syd, Ki fell off his horse!" were the last words he heard before his world momentarily faded to black.

Chapter Seven

"Ki, Ki, wake up." A hand, covered in wool, patted his cheek in a gentle touch at odds with what he knew about the owner. "Ki, please open your eyes so I know you're all right."

His nose twitched as the now-familiar exotic scent filled his nostrils. It was a lot nicer wake-up call than most hangovers punished him with. And right now, this one felt like a grade-A head killer.

He carefully opened one eye to see how bad the world looked. Ki looked up at Syd's face. He was surprised to find concern etched on her lovely features. He thought for sure she'd be disgusted by his behavior. Although he wished he remembered if he had had any fun. That was when he realized that where he lay was very cold. He looked around and saw only snow. How did he get outside?

"What happened?" he croaked, starting to rise up on one elbow. He looked again at the trees and snow. Memory then hit him like a sledgehammer. He'd fallen off his horse and against something very hard and unyielding.

"Don't get up until I can make sure you haven't broken anything." Syd gently pushed him back down.

Pain imploded through Ki's upper body with a vengeance as he shifted. He swore long and hard as the pain seemed to twist viciously through every muscle. Especially his left arm.

"Is he hurt bad?" Heidi's tearful voice asked. She stood just behind Syd looking scared to death. Jamie stood next to her with his arms wrapped around her shoulders in a comforting hug. The three horses' reins dangled from one hand.

"Aw, hell, I broke something, didn't I?" he said between clenched teeth.

Syd quickly ran her hands over his body in a sweep Ki would have ordinarily made some pretty hot statements about and then indulged in a little touchy-feely of his own. Trouble was, there were two children standing nearby and he felt as if the Jolly Green Giant had just finished stomping all over him.

"No, you're lucky. It looks as if you only dislocated your shoulder," Syd assured him, carefully helping him sit up.

"Lucky?" He gritted his teeth against the pain that refused to leave. "You call a dislocated shoulder *lucky?* What would you have said if I'd broken a bone? That I was lucky I hadn't broken my neck?"

"Probably. I mean it, don't worry. I can snap it back for you," she said soothingly. "No problem."

"No!" He was positive he could feel the sweat pop out on his forehead. "Look, there's a hospital not far from here. Just help me up on my horse. We can go

back to the stable, and if you're right, there's no reason why a doctor can't take care of it in no time."

Syd looked surprised at his vehement refusal. She even took a step back.

"Don't be a wuss! It's not as if I haven't done it before. There was one time in one of those Middle Eastern countries that keeps changing its name. I don't remember what it's called now. Anyway, my partner dislocated his shoulder and I popped it back in without any trouble. Just as well, since there wasn't any medical help for hundreds of miles. He hasn't had any problems with it since then."

"I am not a wuss! I'm being pretty damn smart not to let you get your lethal little hands on me," Ki snarled. "Just get me back up on the damn horse, so we can get back to the damn stable, so you can take me to the damn hospital!"

"We'd be better off walking," Syd argued.

Ki closed his eyes for a moment and counted to ten. None of it could disappear, could it? He opened his eyes. They were still standing there with those damn horses in the background, and he was still in pain.

"The kids can't walk that far. *Just get me up on the horse.*" He struggled to his feet, wanting nothing more than to refuse Syd's assistance but having the sense to know he was going to need her.

Syd squatted down on her heels in front of the kids.

"Heidi, I need you to be really good for me," she said in a low voice. "That means I want you to ride with Jamie, so I can keep an eye on Ki. All right?"

Heidi's lower lip trembled dangerously.

"Is it my fault?" she whispered.

Syd smiled and gave her a quick hug. "No, sweetie, although now I think you know not to jump up and down on a horse." She helped Jamie climb onto the pony, then boosted Heidi up in front of him.

"He really hurts," he whispered, looking fearful. "Will he be okay?"

Syd nodded. "He will just as soon as we get him to the hospital. Don't worry."

"Don't worry. Easy for her to say," Ki muttered darkly, staring at his mount's saddle. "She's not the one in pain."

Ki took things one step at a time as he slowly climbed back into the saddle with Syd standing nearby. His lips tightened to a white line as he settled himself in the saddle. When he reached for the reins, Syd already had them in her hand.

"If you're going to be stubborn enough to ride, I'm not taking any chances in your falling off and injuring yourself further," she told him, looping the reins over one hand as she boosted herself into the saddle.

Ki remembered little of the ride back to the stable. He was too busy trying to keep the pain at bay. Along with the shoulder, he felt bruises blooming all along his lower body from falling against that boulder.

When they reached the stable, Syd quickly shouted out their need for help and commandeered one of the hands to assist Ki down.

"Wow, man," the stable hand commented, looping Ki's good arm over his shoulder to help him toward the Jeep. "I did this once. I hurt like the devil for days."

"Thanks a lot," Ki said through gritted teeth. Seeing the look of stark fear on Heidi's and Jamie's faces, he bit back the curses burning his tongue as the younger man carefully secured the seat harness across his chest.

"You just go out to the highway, make a left, and you'll find the hospital about fifteen miles down the road," he told Syd, casting an appreciative gaze over her slender figure.

She gave him a smile that Ki dourly figured warmed the man up for the rest of the day.

"Thanks."

"Ki." A tiny hand gently patted the back of his neck. "When I fall down and get hurt, Auntie Syd kisses it better."

"Yeah, well, this isn't something a kiss can make better," he told Heidi, exerting every ounce of energy so as not to frighten her. Ki would be the first to admit he didn't deal well with pain.

"I did offer to snap it back in for you," Syd reminded him, putting the Jeep in gear.

He stared straight ahead while wishing he had some of Zeke's rotgut. He knew he'd only need a swig of the home brew to banish this pain for all time. "You really want to give those kids a scary education, don't you? Just do me a big favor and avoid the bumps and potholes along the way." He finally closed his eyes and rested against the seat.

With a screech of rubber against asphalt, Syd took off.

Ki felt as if he had barely closed his eyes, and when he opened them again, Syd was pulling into the hospital parking lot and racing for the emergency entrance.

"What did you do? Drive at the speed of light?"

"Close enough. Do you have insurance?" she asked, pulling into a no-parking zone.

He closed his eyes, finding it difficult to think. "Yeah, my card is in my wallet. Right front pocket."

Syd leaned over. "Most men keep their wallet in their back pocket, Jones. Trust you to be different." Her mind raced at lightning speed. "I think it's best I tell them I'm your wife even though it won't be all that easy since I know next to nothing about you. But I've always been good at bluffing my way out of situations."

"Aw, hell," he groaned, keeping his eyes closed. "Can't you tell them you don't know me and you found me by the side of the road?"

"I don't think so, Jones. Now, let's find that card of yours."

Ki was too far gone to appreciate Syd's hand digging around in his pocket. But Syd wasn't.

As she inched her hand in the pocket, she felt the heat of his body against her palm. And as she tucked her hand in deeper, Syd felt something else.

For the first time, she realized her face was burning with embarrassment. And the rest of her body was burning with something a lot more elemental. Syd knew if Ki hadn't been in so much pain and the kids weren't in the back seat, she would have done a lot more than just pull his wallet out of his jeans! Taking a deep breath to still her racing heart, she tucked the wallet in the side pocket of her parka and jumped out of the Jeep.

"Just let me do all the talking," she ordered, pulling open the passenger door.

"I didn't think you'd have it any other way," he muttered, accepting her helping hand.

Syd looked over her shoulder at the kids trailing behind them.

"Just go along with whatever I say," she said softly.

He wasn't so far gone he didn't misunderstand her meaning.

"Oh, my God, what are you going to do?"

Syd didn't bother with further explanations. She was already frantically gesturing to a nurse.

"Please, you have to help him!" she cried out in a thick southern drawl. "He fell and he did somethin' awful to his arm!"

"Oh, hell, she's Scarlett O'Hara again." He groaned, not just from pain.

"Daddy's hurt!" Jamie also cried out, valiantly throwing himself into his role.

"Ma'am, we'll need some information about the patient," the admitting clerk told Syd.

"Then take it from this." Syd dug out Ki's wallet and pulled out the insurance card, handing it to the woman. "He needs to see a doctor now. He's in a lot of pain."

"And he will, but we do have rules here."

Unseen by the others, Syd caught Jamie's eye and gave a little jerk of the head. She figured her bright nephew would understand what she wanted. She was so proud he didn't disappoint her.

Jamie didn't hesitate in pinching Heidi's side. She screamed and would have retaliated with a punch to his stomach, but he grabbed hold of her in a bear hug.

"She's real scared," he told the clerk.

The foursome were the immediate focus of attention by the other waiting patients and visitors. Caught up in the excitement of a captive audience, Heidi continued screaming and Jamie obligingly raised his voice.

Ki winced at the strident sounds pounding through his head. He felt unsteady on his feet.

"Do me a favor and just shoot me now."

For a moment, the nurse looked as if she wanted to do just that. She gestured for Ki to follow her. Syd dug into Ki's wallet and pulled out several bills, handing them to her nephew.

"Here, get her some hot chocolate and something to eat, but make sure the only sugar comes from the hot chocolate," she told Jamie, then raced to catch up with Ki and the nurse. "And don't talk to anyone! I'll be back out as soon as possible."

"Stay with the kids," Ki told her.

"No way. I'm going to make sure you're all right," she told him, quick on his heels. "Jamie's very trustworthy."

Ki was too weary to argue with anyone. Especially when he knew Syd would win. He grimaced as the nurse took his temperature and blood pressure and asked several questions.

"The doctor will be with you in a moment," she told him, casting Syd a suspicious look as she pulled the curtain around the gurney Ki sat on.

"You are really sick," Ki told Syd once they were alone. "I can't believe the stunt you just pulled. You couldn't stay out there with the kids and wait for me, could you? No, you had to go into an Oscar-winning dramatic scene that will have everybody out there talking for days. You have a hell of a method for someone who wants to keep a low profile. You really should think about a film career. You'd be an instant hit."

"No, thanks, everyone knows spies have more fun. Besides, word about our little episode will only last until something more interesting happens. In an emergency room that could be in the next five minutes," she whispered. She touched his hand with her fingertips. "I'm sorry you got hurt. It was really all my fault."

He was surprised by her instant acceptance of blame. "Why? Because my horse spooked and tossed me? It wasn't as if you had tried one of those lethal martial arts moves on me."

She shook her head. "It wouldn't have happened if I hadn't pushed you into going riding with us. If you'd stayed at the cabin working on your book, you wouldn't be in here waiting for a doctor who's probably going to inflict more pain."

Ki had to smile at the idea that he was comforting her for his accident.

"Hey, I'm not mad at anybody. I should have realized I could overbalance myself. The way I look at it is I have a good excuse not to work for a while," he said. He wrapped his good hand around the back of her neck and gently pulled her between his spread legs until her thighs bumped the metal edge of the gurney. "I'm not used to having anyone look out for me. Maybe there's something to be said for being an invalid."

"What's that?" she whispered.

"You'll feel so sorry for me, you won't run away." His warm breath feathered across her lips just before his mouth covered them.

"I'm not running now," she murmured against his mouth.

Syd's lips instinctively parted as Ki's tongue sought entrance. She kept one hand braced against his chest, feeling the warmth of his body against her palm and the slow steady beat of his heart before it began to accelerate.

Ki instantly forgot to worry about where they were or that someone might walk in on them. All that mattered to him was the woman with the responsive mouth. Her lips tasted like honey that was flavored with something dark and sweet. He wanted to take her parka and sweater off. He wanted to sample the rest of her body. He wondered wildly if they could fit on the narrow gurney. He wouldn't mind finding out. He wondered if making love to her would be as sweet as kissing her. Or if it would be hot and wild. He wondered if he could survive the experience.

A low cough warned them they were no longer alone.

Ki slowly lifted his head and turned while Syd stepped back, looking properly embarrassed. He wanted to laugh out loud at the chastened expression on her face. He doubted she'd ever felt embarrassed in her life.

The doctor looked amused at catching them in a compromising position. the nurse standing just behind him looked offended.

"A hurt shoulder usually doesn't require mouth-to-mouth resuscitation," the doctor told them, walking over to Ki's side. "Hello, Mr. Jones. I'm Dr. Waverly. I understand you fell off a horse."

"It was just terrible, Doctor," Syd drawled, fluttering her eyelashes like a proper southern belle. "My darlin's in so much pain. You will be able to help him, won't you?"

"Of course we will," he assured her as he helped Ki take off his shirt. He performed his examination with a minimum of fuss, but with a lot of pain for Ki. "It sounds as if you weren't completely knocked unconscious, though. I'll want X rays to make sure you don't have a concussion. But I don't need X rays to tell you that you have a dislocated shoulder, Mr. Jones."

Syd looked properly stunned at his diagnosis as she tried not to stare at Ki's chest and the bruises already blooming a bright purple along his side.

"Oh, no, is that bad?" Syd asked.

"It can be." The doctor's smile was reassuring as he gazed at Syd with male appreciation. "But I will have to knock him out to snap it back into place."

Ki's mouth fell open. "What do you mean knock me out? Can't you just tell me to grit my teeth and give a yank?"

Syd shot him a look that told him that was what she'd intended to do before he objected.

"It's for the best. When you're aware of what we're going to do, you tend to tense up. With you under general anesthetic, you'll be completely relaxed. Of course, you'll have to wear a sling for a while and take it easy. You were lucky you didn't do a lot of damage. You'd be surprised what some people have done to themselves. Some have even required surgery."

"How about using a local?" Ki demanded. "That'll relax me."

Dr. Waverly shook his head. "Not nearly as effective. No matter what, you'd still feel the need to tense up."

Ki could only think of what was going on as they took X rays and readied him. And while he wouldn't admit it to a soul, he was grateful Syd remained by his side using her breathy southern voice to tell him amusing little stories.

"Don't worry, Mrs. Jones, it won't be long before you can take your husband home," one of the nurses told her as the doctor conferred with a technician. "Now, Mr. Jones, please roll over."

Ki's face betrayed his horror. *"What?"*

"I need to give you an injection." The nurse's expression told him the needle wasn't going in his arm.

"Darlin', it will only hurt for a moment," Syd cooed.

"Go away," he muttered, glaring at her. There was no way he was going to bare his backside to her. At least, not here.

"Now, Mr. Jones, don't you want your wife here with you?" the nurse asked.

"Wife! Ha! She's not my wife. A sane man would have to be knocked out to marry someone like her!"

Syd didn't show any embarrassment by his statement. Instead, she smiled as if this was expected from a man who was rapidly dropping into a deep syrupy pool as the injection took effect.

"Now, darlin', you know very well you promised it was time to give our babies your name," she told him just as he felt the darkness overtake him.

Ki's last words hovered on his lips. Syd was positive she was the only one to hear them.

"Hell, no."

JAMIE AND HEIDI were seated on two chairs set in a corner of the waiting room. Jamie was engrossed in a comic book while Heidi stared at the TV set high up against one wall.

"Where's Ki?" Heidi demanded when she saw Syd striding toward them.

"The doctor just finished fixing his shoulder," she explained, squatting down in front of them. She fingered the comic book detailing mighty space-age warriors and gazed at Jamie with a knowing look.

"I got Heidi hot chocolate and me a Coke," he told her. "We had money left over and we went into the gift shop. I got some comics for her, too." He picked up one of the others in his lap. "And I got change. But you really shouldn't have given me Ki's money."

Syd grimaced. "Yes, my little conscience. I'll repay him every penny. I promise."

"What did they do to Ki?" Heidi cut in.

"They put him to sleep so they can—"

Heidi's eyes widened to the size of small saucers. *"Put him to sleep?"* Syd winced at the strident sound. "Cathy Daniels's kitty was put to sleep and he never *woke up!"*

"Sweetheart, believe me, it's not the same thing at all," Syd swiftly assured her, gently clapping her hand over the little girl's mouth. She managed a brief, apologetic smile to the others seated around them. She sensed she was the object of their glares as if she was the cause for Heidi's noisy distress. "It's like when you take your baby aspirin and you feel sleepy. That's all Ki is doing. He's taking a nap."

Heidi sat up straight and crossed her arms in front of her small body swaddled in her bulky parka. "I'm not a baby."

It was one of those times when Syd felt as if she was swimming against the tide. She spoke softly and quickly in hopes Heidi wouldn't interrupt her again. "I know you're not. It's just a better way of explaining it to you. Remember when you had your cold and I gave you your medicine? After you took it you got real sleepy. Well, that's what happened with Ki. Pretty soon he'll wake up and we'll go back to the cabin. But we have to make sure he doesn't hurt his shoulder any more."

Heidi nodded uncertainly then changed the subject with the frequent regularity girls her age were known for. "I have to go to the bathroom."

"I'm not taking her," Jamie stated. His tone left no room for argument.

Syd shot him a telling look before she straightened up and took Heidi's hand. After asking directions to the ladies' rest room, she led her down the hallway.

"I don't like hospitals," Heidi declared as they made their trek. "They smell funny."

"I'm not too fond of them, either," Syd said absently, pushing the door open. She guided Heidi into a stall and waited for her since she had already learned the little girl preferred to be on her own.

"Hospitals aren't nice. People die in them." Her voice echoed in the tile-lined room.

Syd collapsed against the sink. She blinked back the tears stinging her eyelids and blindly gripped the cold porcelain as if it was a lifeline. She only wished she had some idea what to say to Heidi. All Heidi knew was that her parents were taken to a hospital and they never came out.

"MR. JONES. MR. JONES, can you open your eyes for me?"

Ki didn't find it easy to obey the woman's voice. Not when he felt as if his body was comfortably encased in cotton wool.

"What happened this time?" he asked. At least, that's what he thought he said as he opened his eyes to a slit.

The woman bending over him wore blue surgical scrubs with a stethoscope draped around her neck. She held his wrist between her fingertips and glanced down at her watch.

"While you had your nap the doctor put your shoulder back where it belongs." She smiled. "Your wife is outside. Would you like her to come in?"

He closed his eyes because he doubted he could keep them open much longer. "Do I have a choice?"

She chuckled. "Your kids are pretty worried about you, too. Since you're returning to the land of the living, I'll let your wife finish waking you up."

"Believe me, she's much better at knocking people out than waking them up," he muttered.

He smelled the exotic scent before he felt warm lips against his cheek.

"Not a nice thing to say about the mother of your children, Jones," she whispered against his skin. "How do you feel?"

He couldn't help smiling. He wanted to blame it on the knock-out drops the nurse had given him, but he knew it was Syd. "As if you had just dislocated my shoulder."

"No, darlin', I'm afraid you did that all by yourself," she murmured, giving him another kiss on the cheek. "Now, why don't you try to wake up enough so we can get you out of here?"

He thought about that plush cotton wool nest surrounding him. "I like it here."

Syd smiled. She remembered times when she hadn't wanted to wake up to the real world, either.

"Trust me, one bed bath and you'll be begging to get out of here." She leaned over to whisper in his ear, tickling the rim with the tip of her tongue, "Besides, I can give you a much nicer bed bath at home."

"I'm awake. I'm fine. Let's go."

When Ki was released from the hospital a couple of hours later, his arm was nestled snugly in a sling and he was feeling no pain. He still wanted nothing more than to curl up in a corner and go back to sleep.

Syd nonchalantly signed Ki's name to the paperwork with a signature that was eerily identical to Ki's scrawl.

"Thank you so much for all your help." She smiled at the doctor. "I promise I'll get him right home and into bed."

"Mr. Jones should restrain from any strenuous activity," he told her. "And he should either come back in here in a week or have his own physician check him out. I don't think he did a lot of damage, so he might be one of the lucky ones and not require a lot of physical therapy. But right now, that's hard to say."

Syd leaned over as if confiding a deep dark secret.

"I'll do my best to keep him down, but it won't be easy. He's such a tiger." She uttered a low growl before moving away.

The doctor reached up to wipe the sweat from his forehead as he watched Syd's body glide between the open doors. With a dazed glaze in his eyes, he noticed he wasn't the only male watching her departing figure.

"With that woman around, he probably fell out of bed, dislocating that shoulder, and not off a horse," one of the nurses commented.

"It would be worth it," Dr. Waverly muttered.

"NOW, BE A GOOD BOY and I'll read you a story when I tuck you into bed," Syd told Ki as she pulled the shoulder harness across his chest and secured it.

His smile was decidedly lopsided. "Honey, instead of reading me a story, why don't you think about tucking yourself in bed with me?"

She patted his good shoulder. "We'll discuss it when you're feeling better."

"Believe me, I've never felt better in my life."

Syd walked around to the driver's side and climbed in.

Jamie hung over the front seat and stared at Ki. The older man sprawled bonelessly in his seat, humming under his breath and looking as if he was in a world entirely of his own making.

"What's wrong with him?" Jamie hung over the front seat, so he could look into his aunt's face.

"Painkillers. He'll be back to his real self in the morning. Now, please sit back and buckle up."

Jamie looked at Ki once more before settling back. "I don't know. I think I like him more this way."

Chapter Eight

"Did you ever notice how dark it gets after the sun goes down?" Ki asked as if his question was the beginning of an intellectual conversation. "Look around you. It really gets dark out here. You almost can't see your face in front of your hand." He frowned as he realized his statement didn't sound right. "Hand in front of your face. Hand in front of your face. Yeah, that's it."

Syd was too busy making sure Ki's loose-limbed body didn't throw her off-balance to bother answering. She maneuvered him out of the Jeep and into the cabin.

"I'm out of shape for this," she said, weaving their way to the couch and dropping a limp Ki onto it. "Come on, guys, let's get you outside," she told the dogs. She walked back to the front door and watched them race around for several minutes before they ran back inside and jumped around her, bidding for her attention.

Ki lay sprawled on the couch, his mouth open in a bone-cracking yawn.

"I am really tired." He turned on his side, curled up on the couch and closed his eyes. Bogie promptly jumped onto the couch, climbed onto Ki's hip, curled up in a tight ball and fell asleep.

"Good idea." Syd eyed the easy chair and thought fondly of collapsing onto the comfortable cushions. "I had no idea a leisurely horseback ride could turn into such a catastrophe."

"Are we gonna eat?" Jamie asked plaintively, planting himself in front of her. "I'm starvin'."

"How did Donna Reed manage it all and keep smiling?" she murmured, forcing her leaden body into the kitchen. She took a quick inventory of the cabinets. "Hey, how about macaroni and cheese?"

"Dinosaur macaroni?" Heidi asked in that hopeful voice that implied her request would be granted.

"Sorry, Heidi, it's just your everyday macaroni, but it will taste just the same." Syd filled a pan with water and set it on the stove.

While waiting for the water to boil, she checked quickly on Ki, who was still sleeping peacefully on the couch.

"Can we watch TV?" Jamie asked, picking up the remote control and plopping down on the floor.

"Only if you keep the volume low, so you don't wake Ki up, and not pick anything that will give Heidi nightmares," Syd said absently, as she pressed the back of her fingers against Ki's forehead and brushed back a stray lock of hair. She was pleased to find his skin cool to the touch. Bogie opened one eye, decided she wasn't going to take him off his comfortable perch and went back to sleep.

"I might as well pick the cartoon channel," Jamie muttered, turning the television on and flipping channels.

Syd allowed the kids to eat in front of the television while she munched on some of the macaroni and cheese and kept an eye on Ki. She tried to wake him a couple of times and asked if he preferred to be in bed, but he only smiled at her, puckered his lips in a comic parody of a sloppy kiss and promptly fell back asleep. In the end, she settled for draping a blanket over his shoulders.

"I hope I never dislocate my shoulder." Jamie made a face as he watched Ki's response to Syd shaking his arm.

"I should have just gone ahead and snapped it back in place. He wouldn't have known what was going on until it was all over," she muttered, digging her spoon into the macaroni and eating with little appetite. In the end, she gave most of her meal to Cocoa, who had been eyeing her dish from the moment she had sat down.

By the time Syd washed the dishes and got the kids to bed, she felt so tired, she was ready to drop. Cocoa and Bogie both curled up on her bed as if they decided they were ready for bed, too. Syd went downstairs only to find Ki still sleeping peacefully on the couch. She could see that, while she had been gone, he had somehow managed to struggle out of his jeans and sweater.

"Ki. Ki." She gently shook his shoulder. "Are you sure you don't want to go to bed?"

He opened his eyes. "Sounds great to me, hot stuff. Anything you're interested in, so am I. Come to Daddy." He held his arms out.

She swallowed her laughter at his outrageous invitation. "While you sound so obviously sincere, I doubt you're up to any fun and games tonight."

The drugged glaze in his eyes told her she was right.

"Sure I am." He sat up, the blanket dropping to his waist. He idly scratched his chest. "But first, I have to make a real important call." He looked around the room. "Where's my phone?"

Syd's mouth dropped open in shock as Ki stood up and walked unerringly to the table where he kept his cellular phone in a drawer. It wasn't so much his steady stride that caught her attention as the man dressed in a pair of navy briefs and white T-shirt. The night she had seen him naked was only a blurred memory, although a pleasant one. She could see that reality was so much better than memories. She braced her hip against the back of the couch and watched him with frank appreciation.

"What do you think you're doing?" she asked him.

"I gotta call Tripp," he explained, punching numbers in slow motion.

Syd studied Ki and was convinced he was still in a fog from the painkiller he'd been given before they left the hospital.

"Ki, do you realize what time it is? We have spent the last three-quarters of the day at the hospital. Most normal people are in bed by now, no matter what part of the country."

"I gotta tell Tripp I'm sorry." He punched in three numbers, paused, punched in another and held the phone to his ear. "Hell, why isn't this ringing?"

Syd shook her head in exasperation. She straightened up and walked over. She didn't bother asking for it. She just took the phone out of his hand.

"If people could see you now, they'd wonder how you could write a book. If you don't push enough buttons, the number you call can't ring. Now, please, go lie down."

He made a vain grab for it. "No, I have to do this. I have to tell Tripp I'm sorry for calling Bridget what I did."

She easily kept the phone out of his reach. "What do you mean you have to tell Tripp you're sorry for what you called Bridget?"

"I have to call him. He's one of my best friends, and I called his bride Egghead at the wedding because that was what we used to call her in college, and I told him I couldn't believe he was marrying her," he explained, then went on to further clarify, "I was a little drunk at the time. So he threw me up against a wall. I have to tell him I'm sorry for calling her that and that I know they're happy together. I mean, Tripp wouldn't marry a real dog. He's the one with the good taste."

Syd's shoulders started to shake slightly, then harder with her laughter until she almost couldn't stop. She took several deep breaths to control herself.

"You're lucky he didn't break your nose," she chuckled, holding the palm of her hand against her stomach. "You idiot! You don't say something that dumb. Especially when the man is marrying the woman in question!'' She shook her head. ''Why am I trying to reason with you? You're in LaLa Land because of those pain pills. I doubt you can even understand one thing I'm saying.'' She walked away with the phone in her hand. ''The last thing you need to do is call your friend while you're not in your right mind. Who knows what he might do to you.''

''Hey, that's my phone! You can't take away my phone!'' Ki lurched after her and promptly lost his balance. ''Whoa!''

Syd turned just in time to see Ki's body falling directly at her. Her squeak of dismay was muffled as she fell backward onto the couch with Ki dropping on top of her. She deftly twisted her body so his injured arm was cushioned against her.

He blinked several times.

''Are the kids asleep?'' he whispered.

She licked her lips. ''Dead to the world.''

''The dogs out of the way?''

''Sound asleep.'' Syd was surprised Ki had stayed alert for as long as he had. Judging by his glazed eyes, she sensed he would crash very soon.

His grin was lopsided and very endearing. ''Wanna fool around?''

''What about your phone call to your friend?''

He looked blank. ''What phone call?''

Syd took a deep breath. Clearly, reasoning with the man was not possible. ''Don't you think you should take it easy? You could have done further damage to your arm.''

Ki looked down at his sling as if he couldn't re-member hurting it.

"It looks okay to me."

Syd was finding his weight on her all too pleasur-able. "Ki, let me up."

His grin grew even more lopsided. "I thought we were going to fool around."

"No, you're going to bed. Alone. And I'm going to bed. Alone." She found it more difficult to say than she thought it would be. She wondered if she could be accused of taking advantage of a man under the in-fluence. And if it would prove to be fun.

Ki bent his head and caught Syd's mouth in a deep kiss that ensnared her. She forgot about his injury. She forgot that he was pumped full of pain medication and not entirely in his right mind. She forgot everything but the wicked, wild things this man's mouth was do-ing to hers. Trailing behind those thoughts came more than a few of what his mouth *could* be doing to her if she gave him the high sign.

Syd exhaled a soft sigh into Ki's open mouth when she felt his hand slide under her sweater, fumbling with her bra clasp. She shifted her body to give him easier access when the heat of his hand replaced the cool lace. She pushed his T-shirt up above his waist, so she could feel his bare skin against hers. She lightly scratched her nails across his nipples, smiling when he uttered a soft curse. When she felt his hips pressing against hers, she obligingly opened her thighs so she could easily cradle him. His weight grew heavier, but she didn't mind. Why should she, when the kids were upstairs sound asleep and the adults were downstairs indulging in more than the touchy-feely Ki had teased her about earlier? Right now, that was just fine with her.

"I hope you won't blame this on the painkillers tomorrow," she murmured, drawing his earlobe between her teeth and biting down gently. That was when she realized that he felt heavier than he had a moment ago. And that what she thought was a sexy groan breathed in her ear now sounded more like a soft snore. A soft snore?

"Ki?" She gently pushed on his chest. "Ki?"

All she got for her trouble was another low rumbling snore in her ear.

It took Syd a couple tries before she was able to wiggle her way out from under him.

"Too bad you're not awake to enjoy this," she muttered.

She stood over his prone body, looking down at him with an affection at odds with the frustration screaming through her body.

"Jones, you are such a . . ." She stopped, unable to come up with the right description of the man who was driving her so crazy.

She went into his bedroom and came out with two more blankets and a pillow. She carefully turned him over, making sure his injured arm was carefully nestled against one of the rolled-up blankets and covered him with the other, along with the blanket she'd brought in earlier. Lastly, she slipped his pillow under his head. Before she snapped off the light, she dropped a kiss on his forehead.

"Better luck next time, sport," she whispered against his skin.

Syd got up several times during the night to check on Ki. Each time, she found him still sleeping peacefully and looking as if he hadn't moved. And each time, she thought about crawling under the blanket so he would wake up to more than Bogie tucked in next to him. The small dog had followed her downstairs the first time she came down and decided to stay with the sleeping man.

"Lucky you," she told the dog before she went back upstairs to crawl into her own lonely bed.

"ARE YOU SURE he's not dead?"

"He's not dead, Heidi, so stop asking that!"

"But he looks dead."

"How do you know? Have you ever seen a dead person?"

"No, but he looks dead."

Ki debated whether to keep his eyes closed and listen to Heidi and Jamie discuss his mortality or open them and see if the world on the other side of his eyelids looked as bad as it did on this side.

In the end, he opted for the latter. And almost shouted in fear when he opened his eyes and saw nothing but a tan, fuzzy world. It took a moment for him to realize it was because one of the dogs was lying on the pillow in front of him. Before he could say anything, the dog turned his head and rewarded Ki with a slurp of his tongue.

"This wasn't the kind of good morning kiss I was hoping for," he told Bogie before gently pushing him away. He saw Jamie and Heidi seated cross-legged on the carpet in front of him. Both sets of eyes were focused on him. With the fire crackling merrily in the fireplace in the background, he didn't have any trouble visualizing himself residing in hell.

"Wouldn't you rather watch cartoons?" he croaked.

Jamie turned to Heidi with a smirk on his lips. "See, he's not dead." He turned back to Ki. "Auntie Syd said we weren't supposed to wake you up. And we're supposed to let her know if you wake up." He looked toward the stairs. *"Auntie Syd, he's awake!"*

A pained whimper left Ki's lips as he felt his head start to crack in tiny fissures.

"Please, don't shout," he whispered, holding himself very still so he wouldn't shatter into a million pieces. He doubted Syd would appreciate the mess.

Running footsteps sounded on the stairs, warning him Syd was coming. This time his groan echoed a different kind of pain as he stared up at her.

Dressed in black bike shorts and a tank top, she looked about as good to a dying man as any erotic dream could.

"I was looking over your hot tub earlier this morning," she told him. "I thought you might like to get in it today. It might make you feel better."

Only if you're in it with me, he thought. "That sounds great, thank you."

"Would you like some breakfast?"

Did I have you in my arms last night or was it just a drug induced dream?

"It sounds good."

"Bacon and eggs okay?"

Only if I can't feast on you.

"Fine."

Syd looked at Ki for a long, wordless moment as if she'd read his inner thoughts.

"You just stay here and relax. I'll bring your food, coffee and some juice in here."

Was it Ki's imagination or were Syd's hips swaying just a tad more than usual as she headed for the kitchen?

"You were really funny last night," Heidi thought to inform him.

He kept his attention directed toward the kitchen. "Was I?"

"Auntie Syd said it was 'cause the doctor gave you a shot," Jamie explained, focusing on the TV screen where Wile E. Coyote was still trying to catch the elusive Roadrunner and losing the battle when an anvil dropped on his head.

Heidi's strident giggles tore through Ki's head.

"Heidi, please don't do that," he moaned, dropping back onto the pillow.

"Heidi, remember what I told you. No yelling. No screaming. We remain quiet this morning because Ki doesn't feel well." Syd walked in holding a coffee mug. She gently nudged Ki with her knee and sat on the edge. "Here, this might help." She held the mug to his lips.

He gulped down the caffeine, sighing with relief.

"Thank you," he whispered.

"Painkiller hangovers are never any fun," she murmured.

He now felt his face wouldn't split in two if he smiled. "You're right about that. But then, this whole week has been a surprise for me. If nothing else, you haven't made this past week boring."

Syd glanced quickly at the kids to make sure they were watching television instead of watching them. She carefully placed her hand on his blanket-covered hip.

"If you want to get up, I suggest you do it while Heidi is looking elsewhere," she suggested softly. "She's already seen much more of you than a five-year-old girl should see of the male anatomy, and I'll have enough questions to answer in the coming years without having to start now."

He thought of their first unorthodox meeting. "I was only showing off for you."

"And you did it very well." She took her time straightening up. "I'll hold your food until you come back out."

Ki headed for his bedroom.

"When Ki goes in the hot tub, can we go in, too?" Jamie asked, excited at the idea of swimming outside when there was snow all around. "We'd be real careful and not bump his arm."

Syd uttered a soft sigh. "Are you sure you wouldn't rather take a nap?"

"A *nap?*"

She held up her hands in surrender and almost had coffee splashing all over her when the mug tipped a little. "It was a joke, Jamie."

He scowled at her. "Some of your jokes aren't very funny, Auntie Syd. All I asked is if we can go in the hot tub, too?"

Syd cocked her ear as she heard the shower running in the next room. It wasn't until recently she started wondering how parents managed to have any kind of love life. She couldn't exactly send the kids next door to play for a few hours while Auntie Syd and Uncle Ki played another type of game in the hot tub.

"We'll see."

"That means no," he muttered, pulling his video game into his lap and switching it on.

Syd waited until she heard the shower turn off before going back into the kitchen and fixing Ki's breakfast. When she later took the bacon out of the microwave, she could hear Jamie and Heidi chattering to Ki and his low-voiced replies.

She told herself she should feel guilty for basically barging in on him and refusing to leave. He had all the right in the world to demand she leave, and yet he hadn't exercised that right. In the process, she'd turned his life upside down, interfered with his creative processes and as a bonus gotten him injured so badly he had to go to the hospital.

"It's a wonder he didn't throw me out that first night," she murmured, feeling a prickling sensation along the back of her neck. A sure sign she wasn't alone in the room.

"Why would I do that? If I threw you out, I'd have to cook." Ki dropped a kiss on her shoulder. "Good, you didn't try to kick me this time."

She smiled. "That's because I knew you were there."

His breath ruffled her hair. "Was I hallucinating last night thanks to the doctor's happy juice or did we get a little intimate with each other?"

"A *little* intimate is the right way to phrase it," she agreed.

"Not a lot intimate?" He sounded disappointed.

Syd backed up until her bottom was nestled in the cradle of his hips. A quick sideways glance and the sound of giggles from the living told her the kids were still engrossed in cartoons.

"Obviously, I wasn't fascinating enough for you. You fell asleep just when it was getting—" she paused a beat "—interesting."

Ki groaned. His good arm snaked its way around her waist and held her tightly against him.

"So I didn't get to count all the freckles on your body?"

She turned around in his embrace and shook her head.

"I didn't even get to find out if you have freckles anywhere else on your body?"

Syd's lips twitched. Again, she shook her head.

"Did you get to find out if I had any freckles?" Ki asked hopefully.

She slowly ran her tongue across her bottom lip. "Are we talking about that crescent-shaped scar on your left hip?" she whispered, placing her hand in the exact spot.

"Yeah," he exhaled.

She traced the area with her forefinger. "Slightly raised, a little over an inch long? The kind that looks as if you were caught up in wire?"

His eyes started to glaze over. "Yeah."

She frowned in momentary thought. "No, I don't recall seeing anything like that."

It took Ki a moment to recover.

"Lady, you are something else." He chuckled.

"I try. I really try. Now, why don't you sit down while I finish fixing your breakfast?" She gave him a gentle push.

Ki sat at the table, turning so his arm cradled in the sling wouldn't be accidentally bumped.

"You'd probably be more comfortable in the living room."

He shook his head. "Why should I watch cartoons when I'd rather watch you?"

Syd paused in her movements. "This is getting complicated."

"Is it?"

She nodded. "We've been thrown together in an unusual manner, so our hormones are having a field day. Except, there's two kids around to keep them in check. The attraction's there, but I don't dare give in to it and you shouldn't."

"Why shouldn't I?" He was curious to hear this answer.

Syd turned around, leaning back against the counter.

"Because it won't be long before the kids and I are gone," she said quietly. "I've stayed here longer than I should, but with Christmas coming, I didn't want to

move them around too much. Heidi's having enough
trouble believing Santa Claus will find her.''

"You said there was no reason for your boss to
track you down here," he argued. "If there isn't, then
there's no reason why you can't stay here as long as
you like.''

"That's true, but Leo is famous for never doing
anything in a logical manner. To make it worse, he
knows I'm anything but logical. What's good is, I've
had my time to myself and I know he can't force me to
go back to the agency. I guess my taking off the way I
did was a form of rebellion. I didn't have to worry
about answering the phone to hear his voice or opening the door to find him standing there. But now, I
have to consider Jamie's schooling. I can't keep him
out much longer.''

"You wouldn't even go back to teach?''

She laughed. "The last thing they want me to do is
teach. I filled in for one of the instructors one day and
I almost traumatized the entire class. It was put in my
personnel jacket that I was never to be allowed near a
training class again, no matter how badly they needed
someone to teach. Ki, we're not exactly your typical
male-meeting-female in a bar and getting to know each
other. There's a lot going on around us that we can't
ignore. And I don't mean all those hidden signals between us, either. You know it and I know it.''

Ki watched Syd, saw the emotion clouding her eyes
and knew if he wasn't careful he might lose something very important. Funny he would even think that
way. After all, he'd never had any complaints about
his way of life before. Not having anyone else to worry

about, the ability to pick up and take off for that next book subject, were the things he liked best about his work. Syd had raised an issue he didn't think was meant for him. Still, he wasn't crazy enough to pass up an opportunity that could turn out to be the chance of a lifetime.

"There's no reason why we can't relax and enjoy what we have." he suggested. "You should be grateful we're not typical people. It wouldn't be half as much fun."

He wasn't sure he saw relief flickering in her eyes from his words. But he sure hoped it was.

Chapter Nine

"Tell me about the man you're writing about."

Ki looked up from his study of the papers scattered all around him. While his arm still ached, it wasn't as bad as it had been first thing that morning. He hated the frustration of tangling himself up in the sling and only kept it close by if he moved around. The doctor said just to make sure not to move his arm too. Sitting here working one-handed was awkward, but he was grateful his injuries weren't worse.

Syd had mentioned taking the kids out for the morning and he decided that was as good a time as any to get back to work. After all, it was why he'd come out here.

He slipped off his reading glasses and set them to one side.

"You really want to hear about Thomas Baskin? He isn't a very nice man. Not exactly the kind of person you'd want to meet in a single's bar."

Syd's lips curved in amusement. "I didn't say I wanted to date him. Don't worry, Ki, I've had a *little* experience with the seamier side of life. Telling me about him won't give me nightmares.''

He inclined his head in acknowledgement of her statement. ''Where are the kids?'' He knew it wouldn't be a good idea for Heidi or Jamie to overhear his words.

''Heidi was tired out from our morning spent at Kiddie's Ville, and Jamie's in the living room playing his video games.'' Syd dropped onto the end of Ki's bed, dislodging papers and photographs. She picked up one of the photographs taken at one of the murder scenes and studied it carefully. She shook her head.

''Obviously, this guy doesn't like women very much.'' She set it down. ''So tell me about him.''

''Why?''

She shrugged. ''You said you were having trouble putting things in place. You've spent a lot of time going over your notes and looking at photos and not as much time at the computer as you'd like. Maybe if you talk to me about Baskin, what you've learned about him and what you hope to show in your book, it might help you put things in perspective. I used to wish I had someone to talk things over with when it got rough.''

Ki's writer's instincts instantly took over. He had an idea if anyone's life would make a good book, Syd's experiences would. ''Like what?''

Syd looked off into space. ''Oh, there was a time in Madrid when I was following a well-known arms dealer who was planning a huge sale of weapons to a small Middle Eastern country.'' The memory still made Ki's blood run cold. ''The thing was, he frequented mens' clubs and it wasn't all that easy for me to get close to him. The man I usually partnered with was off on another assignment since it wasn't felt that both of us were needed.''

Ki picked up his pen and started doodling on his legal pad. ''You partnered with a guy?''

She nodded. ''Mike was great. We worked together for about three years and got to the point where we could read each other's minds.''

He felt the burning pangs of something he wasn't all that familiar with: jealousy.

''You were real close, huh?''

Syd reached over the side of the bed and picked up Bogie, who promptly draped himself across her lap and closed his eyes. Cocoa jumped up and walked with canine unconcern over Ki's papers until he reached Ki's pillow and curled up on the smooth percale.

''Why don't you make yourself at home,'' he growled at the dog, who looked at him with large brown eyes then closed them.

''Sorry, I've sort of spoiled them,'' Syd explained.

''If you're out of the country so much, why did you get a dog?'' he asked. ''And then get a second one?''

She shook her head. ''I guess it was because I walked into a pet store and there was this tiny brown ball of fur who begged me to take him home. I was in the middle of my vacation, and I think, even then, I was considering leaving. I got Bogie because I didn't want Cocoa to be lonely. They stayed with Shane and Jenny when I was away on an assignment.''

''With Mike,'' Ki muttered, wondering just how close she was to her partner.

Syd cocked her head to one side. She'd tied her hair up in a ponytail on one side of her head. As always, she was dressed simply in leggings, heavy socks and a sweater that was cropped at her waist. But as always, it was her scent that he felt described her best. Exotic, erotic and utterly feminine.

Ki was fascinated with the seductive view of bare skin revealed each time she moved her shoulders. He bet she looked as sexy in casual clothes as she would in an evening gown.

"You sound as if you don't like Mike," she commented. "And you haven't even met him."

"Hey, if you like him, he must be a great guy," he protested with little sincerity. "I'm sure he's a real prince. An all-right guy. The kind of guy everyone likes."

"And very happily married."

Ki's mouth closed on whatever else he was going to say. "Married?"

She nodded. "He got married not long after our last assignment. He's now a supervisor over agents in Western Europe and has a lovely office in D.C. Last I heard his wife was pregnant." She leaned over. "And Ki..." She waited until he looked at her. "There was never anything between us. I considered Mike another brother and he saw me as a younger sister. While we had to work closely together, and even in what could be construed as an intimate situation, we never became intimate."

"But you could have," he pressed.

"We could have, but we chose not to. There haven't been all that many men in my bed," she said candidly. "Mainly because of what I did for a living. It wasn't the greatest way to meet men. When I did, I couldn't divulge my profession. I did not go to bed with the enemy to gain information, and I wouldn't have gone to bed with my partner unless there was a mutual strong feeling between us." She shrugged. "As it was, we knew a love affair could ruin our concentration in crucial times. Would it make you feel better if I gave you a rundown on the men I've slept with? I don't know what exactly you want to know, so you'll have to give me an idea. Vital statistics? A rating as to how they were in bed, what we did and what I liked them doing to me? What?" she pushed. Her eyes glittered with icy blue lights. "Come on, Ki. What do you want to hear?"

Ki started to lunge for her, but Bogie's raised head and low warning growl stopped him.

"Dammit, I don't want a list of your lovers," he growled, pushing the papers off his lap. "Look, you talk about some guy you must have worked with day and night and how you read each other's minds, so it's natural I'd think the two of you were also great in the sack."

Her lips parted in a surprised oh. "You're jealous."

Ki fidgeted under her wide-eyed regard. "Damn straight I'm jealous," he grudgingly admitted. "I'm jealous of any bastard who's been in bed with you when I haven't yet."

"Be careful, Ki. Someone might think you really care."

He shook his head at her gentle teasing. "Sometimes it gets to you. Just like the mumps."

Syd looked down at the dog sleeping in her lap. She ran her hand across his back in a slow sweep. She could feel the tension building. After all, she and Ki were sitting on his bed.

One child was asleep; the other was engrossed in a video game that Syd knew could keep him entertained for hours.

Who would know if she edged both dogs out the door and closed it after them? Unless the dogs started barking and howling or Heidi woke up and came looking for her or... The list was endless. She slowly lifted her head.

"Tell me about Thomas Baskin."

Ki knew she wasn't ignoring the tension between them. She was only putting it on hold for a while. Which was fine with him. The prospect of kids walking in at any moment was more than a little daunting.

"Thomas Baskin is very good-looking, very charming and very lethal," he began. "He loves women enough to marry them and hates them enough to kill them without a second thought."

"How many?"

"Don't you read the papers? He was on national news for I don't know how many weeks."

"I gave up CNN for Nickelodeon. How many women?"

"The cops were able to nail him for seventeen murders in ten states. He admitted he lost count a long time ago and states there's even more than that. Authorities are still going through old records of unsolved homicides in those states where a wife was killed and the husband wasn't implicated. He might have kept up with it longer if he'd used a spy disguise kit like yours."

Syd gave a low whistle. "Nice guy. I wonder how many women out there are grateful he didn't ask them for a second date."

"Quite a few, according to the tabloid TV shows." He sorted through his notes and picked out one sheet. He handed it to her. "This is what he told me about the first woman he killed."

Syd scanned the sheet. "I know there have been husbands who have killed their wives because they think she's seeing another man and they're afraid she's going to leave them. And some of them find out later they're wrong. Obviously, Baskin thought he was in the right every time or I would think he'd have stopped."

"I don't think he ever would have stopped," Ki said, getting into the crux of the story. "That's what I want to tell my readers. This man didn't just enjoy killing. He enjoyed killing women he was married to. He never thought of harming a woman he only dated. They didn't mean as much to him on an emotional level. But his wives meant a lot to him. He quickly learned his role as a grieving widower had the women on him like fleas on a dog. It wasn't long before he remarried and went through all the same insecurities."

"An addiction," Syd murmured. "He was hooked."

Ki's eyes lit up. "Yeah. He couldn't stop because he was addicted to killing his wives. Funny, I didn't think secret agents could zero in on your ordinary serial killers."

"You, of all people, know that serial killers aren't ordinary. Besides, I've always been fascinated by a killer's mind," she admitted. "That arms dealer I followed in Madrid used to get his jollies from killing women in not very nice ways. The more pain they revealed, the more pleasure he got from it."

"Bet he had a hell of a time getting a second date from a woman," Ki quipped, utilizing the dark humor known in any kind of work dealing with the horrors of human nature.

"That's what Mike said. I figured the creep only got lucky through personal ads."

"He's still around?"

Syd shook her head. "He made a big mistake by taking out what turned out to be the sister of a rival dealer. It seems her brother had kept her safe by using another name and he took great care when visiting her. Rumor had it she had a fight with him over something and she knew Ramon was her brother's biggest rival. She just had no idea about Ramon's little quirks. His idea of a private party put her in the hospital where she had to have extensive plastic surgery on her face and chest area. She was later moved to a private nursing home for intensive counseling. She couldn't handle it and later committed suicide. Her brother had Ramon picked up and he personally skinned him alive," she said matter-of-factly.

Ki had to admit he was impressed. "Sweetheart, you ran in some pretty tough circles."

"I told you. I was a danger junkie. For me, walking that fine line was more fun than skydiving."

He winced at her idea of fun. Ki considered himself a freewheeling guy, but skydiving wasn't exactly near the top of his list of things to do.

"Maybe I should have you talk to Baskin. Although, you two would probably compare notes."

"I don't think he'd be all that impressed with me. I don't kill my men. Good ones are too difficult to come by." Syd shifted her position, curling her legs under her. Bogie moaned as she moved him, then fell back asleep.

Ki's lips twitched. "*Come* by?"

"Don't look for something that isn't there, Jones," she chided. "Now, be good. I came in here to help you with your book. Let's talk about Baskin's addiction to killing his wives. Was there a particular point in the marriage when he felt the urge? Did a little voice sound off inside his head? Or did his wife just happen to say the wrong thing one night, which set him off? Maybe she didn't have dinner ready on time. There has to be a very cold side to his nature that allowed him to get away with it as long as he did. After all, he was hardly ever considered the police's prime suspect, even though it's usually the spouse who's under suspicion first. What was so special about him?"

"He was so sincere about his grief for his dead wife, the police automatically believed him," he replied. "I talked to one of the detectives who had questioned him after one of the first murders. He told me he usually suspects the husband first thing, but Baskin was so horrified and grief-stricken he only felt sorry for the guy. When Baskin moved out of the area a few months later, no one thought anything about it. They figured he just wanted to get away from the memories. The fact that he walked away with a half million dollars from her insurance policy didn't even occur to them. This cop is a seasoned veteran, a man who's seen everything. But even he was fooled by Baskin. That's how good he is.''

"Then say so," Syd said simply. "Tell your readers that, unfortunately, the guy who they think is Mr. Right could be Mr. Wrong in the worst way. While many women want a husband and a home and children, they have to know there are some men out there who aren't what they need. Point out that Baskin's wives weren't insecure women just looking for a man.''

"You're very good at this.''

She preened under his compliment. "It's just a different point of view, that's all.''

"And a good one." He leaned across the papers and planted a quick kiss on her lips that quickly warmed to more.

Syd leaned into his kiss, then enjoyed his alternate nibbles and murmurs.

"Auntie Syd, Heidi's up and she's yellin' 'cause she can't find her blue socks!" Jamie shouted.

Syd opened her eyes at the same time she felt Ki's hand slide away from her breast.

"Tell you what, handsome, I'll meet you at the hot tub later tonight and do something about that problem of yours," she whispered, audaciously patting the front of his jeans before she got off the bed.

After a saucy smile and lips pursed in an airy kiss, she was out of the room with Cocoa and Bogie on her heels.

Ki took a deep breath, realizing too late he had inhaled the lingering scent of Syd's perfume. His body tightened further to an unbearable arousal.

"It can't happen soon enough," he muttered, carefully making his way off the bed and heading for the bathroom. Right now, he needed an ice-cold shower.

SYD QUICKLY LEARNED that it wasn't easy to choreograph a seduction when children were around. Especially children who, for the first time in days, didn't start winding down during dinner.

"How come we don't have any dessert?" Jamie asked as he ate the last bite of chicken.

"Because we don't have anything in the house," Syd replied.

"Can't we have ice cream?" Heidi begged, brightening up at the idea of a treat. She lifted pleading eyes to Ki. "Can we, Ki? Can we go for ice cream? Please?"

He knew he should tell her she should ask Syd. He knew he should just flat-out say no. But there was something about her eyes, the same vivid blue shade as her aunt's, that was instantly turning him into putty. He turned to Syd, sending her a silent plea.

"Heidi, don't you think it's too cold to eat ice cream?"

The little girl shook her head back and forth, then quickly switched her attention back to Ki. "Chocolate chip ice cream is my favorite," she confided, fluttering her eyelashes at him the way only a five-year-old girl can and get away with.

"Anything with chocolate in it is your favorite," Jamie jeered.

Heidi spent a scant second glaring at her brother before turning her charm on Ki again. "I bet it's your favorite, too," she said softly.

He looked at Syd. "You gotta give her credit for persistence. Talk about a charmer."

"Sugar, especially at the end of the day, means hyper," Syd said succinctly.

"It can't be that bad," he wheedled. "Come on, let's see where we can find the little lady chocolate chip ice cream. My treat." He flashed Syd a grin that was decidedly predatory. "I'm in the mood for something sweet."

"Yay!" Heidi bounced up and down, unaware of the tension roiling between the two adults, although Jamie looked from one to the other as if sensing something was happening and he wasn't too sure he liked it.

Syd set her fork down on her plate with a decided clink. "You wouldn't rather watch a video that will get them all relaxed and drowsy?" she suggested.

By now, Ki was feeling important under Heidi's hero worship. "Let's give them a treat, Syd," he urged. "They've been really good today. There's a great ice cream place not far from here. What do you say?"

She shot him a look that seemed louder than the kids' excited shouting as they jumped up and ran for their coats.

Since his shoulder felt better, Ki offered to drive when they reached the Jeep.

"I can disengage a simple car alarm," he told Syd as she held up a small remote device. She had tucked her hair up under the navy knit cap again.

"Not like this one." She punched in a series of buttons, then waited until two short beeps alerted her the alarm was disengaged. "Okay." She handed him the keys.

"Pretty fancy alarm for a single mother driving a Jeep," he teased, opening the passenger door for her and the rear doors for the kids who quickly scrambled aboard. "Someone would think you were carrying something dangerous in there." His laugh abruptly shut off at her innocent expression. His arm quickly shot out to bar her climbing inside the vehicle. She looked up, surprise written on her face. "What do you have in this truck?" he hissed.

Syd looked over her shoulder. "Two children."

"Cut the crap, Syd. What is in this truck?" he asked in a fierce voice.

She smiled and reached up to pat his cheek. "Don't worry about it, Ki." She slipped under his arm and climbed inside. "Are we going or not?"

His first reaction was to say no. Until he looked at Jamie's and Heidi's expectant faces. There was no way in hell he could ruin that. He uttered a curse and slammed Syd's door before stalking around the front of the Jeep. He was afraid even to think what might be hidden in the rear. He considered sneaking out later for a search, but after seeing the complicated alarm system she had for the truck, he admitted it would be fruitless.

"Ki, will the ice cream store have chocolate chip ice cream?" Heidi asked during the drive.

"Honey, every good ice cream store has chocolate chip ice cream, and the store we're going to is a very good one." His mind still raced with possibilities. Drugs were instantly ruled out. He couldn't imagine her transporting stolen goods such as rare artworks or jewels. That definitely wasn't her style. Not to mention he couldn't imagine she would do anything illegal.

What did that leave? His writer's mind asked. *What kind of scum has she dealt with in the past?*

As the answer wrote itself in big block letters on the blackboard in his brain, Ki's foot instantly slipped off the accelerator and stomped the brake.

"Ki!" Syd grabbed the dashboard as the Jeep began to slide across the road. Luckily, there was no oncoming traffic and he was able to get the truck back under control.

He pulled over to the side of the road and turned to stare at her.

She stared back and didn't look all that happy. "What were you trying to do? Kill us all?"

He opened his mouth, fully prepared to demand a few answers. Before he could say anything, he noticed two small faces out of the corner of his eye. He snapped his mouth shut and turned back to the steering wheel.

"Nothing," he said shortly, putting the truck in gear and slowly driving down the road. "Not a thing."

"Are we still going for ice cream?" Heidi voiced the fear uppermost in her mind.

Ki concentrated on the dark road ahead of them. "Yes, Heidi, we're still going."

"I'm surprised an ice cream shop would be open this time of year," Syd commented, more to break the silence than because she was curious.

"Tourists make it this far out of Tahoe, especially if they're looking for more than just the casinos or shows," Ki replied. "It used to be a shopping center but eventually went broke. Somebody came up with the idea of turning it into sort of a gigantic food park, and it wasn't long before it took off. You name what kind of food you're in the mood for and you'll find it there."

"Too bad I didn't know about it sooner."

"Since we haven't suffered from food poisoning so far, I don't think we need to worry about eating out," Ki told her.

"Spies have ways of making food more interesting," she said under her breath, earning her a killing glare from Ki. "Wow!" She let out a soft breath when Ki pulled into a left-turn lane.

Silvery foil balls hung from each lamp, and gaily colored lights were strung between them. A giant Santa waved from his sleigh set on top of the center building. At one end was what looked like a gingerbread house and a sign announcing Santa's hours.

"Talk about food wonderland," Syd commented.

"Santa's here!" Heidi said excitedly.

"Honey, he's only here during the daytime," Syd explained, privately vowing to bring the little girl back during the day to visit with Santa.

"Pizza, chicken, Chinese," Jamie said, scanning the brightly-lit signs. "We shoulda had dinner here."

Syd reached over her shoulder and playfully tickled his leg, which was all she could reach.

"If you're complaining, I'll happily let you do the cooking tomorrow."

"You know I can't cook!" He giggled.

"Good thing for us you can't. Who knows what you'd whip up," she teased. Syd turned around as Ki pulled up in front of the Mountain High Ice Cream Factory. A familiar logo on the store next door caught her eye. A soft "oh" escaped her lips.

"Sweet Treat," she whispered in what sounded like awe. Before Ki could walk around to the passenger side, she'd hopped out and opened the door for Heidi. "It's heaven."

He looked confused by her interest. "What? The candy shop?"

Syd shook her head. "Ki, we are not talking about just a candy shop. We are talking Sweet Treat. The *ultimate* candy shop. They're the only ones that make Brown Sugar Creams." Just staring at the shop made her mouth water with anticipation.

Ki slung an arm around her neck and steered her back to the ice cream shop.

"Careful, killer, you're drooling on the sidewalk," he growled in her ear as he pushed open the glass door and almost dragged her inside.

Heidi and Jamie immediately ran over to the display counter to press their noses against the glass while studying the large selection of ice cream flavors. A singer lamenting Grandma being run over by a reindeer blared over the loudspeaker.

Syd seriously thought about socking Ki in the arm. Hard. "You don't understand. Brown Sugar Creams are the absolute best candy around. There is nothing to compare with them. There were months when I couldn't get them and all I could do was fantasize about gorging myself on them."

"Fine, if it will make you feel better, we'll stop by on our way out and pick up a few so you won't freak out in the middle of the night because you're going through some crazy withdrawal." He shook his head in amazement. "I can't believe it. All this fuss about candy."

"That candy is better than sex!" Syd declared, unaware her voice had grown louder with each word.

At that same moment the music stopped and all talk was suspended as the customers' attention was riveted on Syd. Undaunted by what could be considered an embarrassing remark, she merely smiled back.

Her knit cap had slid sideways, revealing falling strands of copper-penny hair brushing her shoulders. Even dressed in a heavy jacket and the dark cap, she looked lovely in his eyes. He also couldn't stop thinking of how she might look in the hot tub, with nothing but steam surrounding her.

He wondered if the kids could be persuaded to eat their ice cream in the Jeep on the way back to the house, and if they could be hustled right off to bed before they had any idea what hit them.

"Sweetheart, you have a very unique way of keeping a low profile." Ki dragged her over to the counter where Jamie pointedly refused to look at them.

"She does this all the time when she sees that candy store," Jamie said, barely moving his lips. "Dad said that candy made her nuts."

Ki noticed several men looking at Syd with the kind of grins on their faces that said they were more than willing to show her sex could be better than candy.

"No, Jamie, I'd say she was nuts long before that candy came into her life."

"Chocolate chip! The man said they have chocolate chip ice cream!" Heidi grabbed Ki's hand. "And he said he can put hot chocolate sauce on it, too! I asked 'im. And they have peppermint ice cream 'cause it's a Christmas ice cream! He said peppermint's what candy canes are."

"Terrific. A sugar high before bedtime. Tonight, *you* can have the pleasure of putting them to bed," Syd declared, hoping the kids would make Ki suffer as much as she had the evening she made the supreme mistake of giving them chocolate cake before bedtime.

Ki felt as if he could do no wrong. "Fine, then you can see how it should be done. Sugar high. Buzz words. That's all they are." He shook his head. "How difficult can it be? You just have to be firm with them. If you show them who's boss, you don't have any trouble with them."

"Of course not," Syd said gravely, although deep down she wanted to explain she'd learned the hard way that parenting wasn't as easy as he was making it out to be.

Ki didn't even stop to think that he sounded very much like a father instead of a man who was determined that home, hearth and family wasn't for him. If he had realized it, he probably would have run for the nearest border. But then, if he stopped long enough to look at Syd's smile, bask in Heidi's little-girl awe and laugh with Jamie, he probably wouldn't have even tried to walk away.

Chapter Ten

"Ki, Jamie's makin' funny noises again and he says there's a dinosaur under my bed! Make him stop!"

Until tonight, Ki had no idea an adult man could shudder with horror at the sound of a child's voice saying his name. Until he heard it for what was probably the hundredth time since they'd arrived back at the cabin an hour earlier.

Syd had gone upstairs earlier to supervise the two kids' baths while Ki remained downstairs. He used that time to pour two glasses of wine. He hummed under his breath as he pulled off the tarp covering the hot tub and turned on the heater in anticipation of a special bath for him and Syd.

Ki held back a sigh as he forced himself up off the couch. After Syd had come downstairs, she made herself comfortable by plopping on the couch and swinging her legs over the couch arm with her wineglass within easy reach on the floor. He spun around in time to catch her fleeting smirk as Heidi's plaintive voice floated downstairs.

"Don't say it," he warned.

She looked up, wide-eyed. "What are you talking about, Ukiah?"

"You know very well what." He sent her a murderous glare.

"Ki, I haven't said a word. I didn't say anything when you told Heidi there was no reason she couldn't have her ice cream on a brownie with hot fudge on top, did I?" Syd said, bestowing her most serene smile on him. "And I didn't say anything when you let Jamie have a second dish."

"No, but you have that smirk on your face as if you're enjoying what's happening up there." He started to advance on her.

"Ki!"

"And to think I took you in that candy shop afterward so you could pick up those damn sugar things," he muttered, turning to stomp up the stairs.

"Brown Sugar Creams," she called after him.

After darkly informing Jamie if he made funny noises again, Ki would look into a muzzle, and after checking under the bed again at Heidi's insistence to make sure there weren't any monsters there, he escaped downstairs.

"Okay, you win. You were right. Sugar turned them into children from hell. Are you happy now?" he asked, panting. "We're going to sit here and pray they go to sleep in the next ten minutes. Then we're heading for the hot tub." His eyes blazed with the idea of a playtime that was more adult in nature.

Syd leaned over the side of the couch to pick up her wineglass. "What about the kids?"

"They can use the hot tub during the day. After dark is for adults only." He held up his hand in a silencing gesture. "Listen . . . I don't hear Heidi yelling or Jamie making those snorting noises. See, I told you they'd quiet down."

Syd found herself enjoying this new side of Ki. For a man who acted almost like Scrooge around kids, he was showing he could maneuver them as well as any parent could.

"Gee, I feel just like Carol Brady transported into the nineties," she murmured.

Ki leaned over, placing a hand on either side of her shoulders. "You think this is funny, don't you?"

"Uh-huh."

"If you laugh, you will ruin the mood I am trying so hard to set up here," he said with quiet deliberation. "I'm talking major seduction. You have had me hot and bothered for many a day, lady. I want us to do something about it."

She was polite enough not to laugh, but she couldn't stop smiling. "But it is funny, Ki. You honestly think you have Jamie and Heidi in control and you don't. I learned real fast that if I had let down my guard for longer than thirty seconds, they'd have me handcuffed to the bed."

"Sounds a little kinky, but I'm game to try it." He suddenly snapped his fingers as if he had just gotten a brainstorm. "Say, do you have any handcuffs stashed away in the Jeep?"

Most men would have been ground into dust by the look Syd shot him. Ki wasn't most men.

"Don't even think about it, Jones." She uncurled her legs and stood up, angling her body until it was flush against his. She tilted her head back so she could look him straight in the eye. "I could hurt you real bad, Jones," she said huskily, lightly bumping her hip against his. "My training goes well beyond standard self-defense. I could create levels of pain you can't even imagine."

Ki didn't misunderstand her meaning. This wasn't about hurting him emotionally. She was using a siren's call to seduce him. And he wasn't immune to her provocative song.

As he stared into her fiery blue eyes, he felt the heat travel through his body and settle smack-dab in the center. There was no denying his body was answering her primitive call.

"I'm starting to get a handle on your moves, Taylor," he countered, taking up the verbal challenge. "You might not have it so easy next time you get tough with me."

Syd trailed her fingers down his uninjured arm, then took his hand and wrapped her fingers around his wrist. Her fore and ring fingers rested against his skin.

"Let me show you my softer side," she murmured, gently pressing against certain nerves. Ki immediately felt the tingle alerting him he was losing feeling in that hand. "Or I can get tough." She lifted his palm to her lips and pressed a kiss in the center.

Whatever Ki was expecting, that wasn't it. He breathed in, uttering a sharp curse as her slightly parted lips burned her brand into his skin.

"Which do you prefer, Ki?" she whispered against his palm.

His laughter was raw in his throat. "You are good, very good."

She looked up under the cover of her lashes. "Of course. I'm the best."

At that moment, Ki couldn't have cared less if Jamie and Heidi were sitting right there in the room. All he knew was that Syd had begun a fire burning deep inside him. A fire he knew only she had the power to quench.

"The kind of danger you're playing with now isn't all that easy to get out of," he said raspily.

She shrugged off his warning as she continued to nibble on his palm.

"You forget, Jones. Danger is my business."

He freed his hand and planted that and his other hand on her hips, drawing her even closer against him.

"Then why don't we see how much trouble we can get into."

Their breaths mingled as their mouths melded. Tongues curled around each other. Bodies twisted and turned in an attempt to get closer. Respiration grew labored, harsh and irregular as their mutual arousal intensified.

Syd almost wrapped her body around Ki's in an attempt to get as close as possible to him. She was taking a chance. She knew it. After all, Ki had clearly stated that he was a loner. And she had the kids to think about. Was it a good idea for them to get well and truly involved? Was it a good idea if they ignored such a golden chance? She knew the answer even before it sounded in her brain.

Syd lifted heavy-lidded eyes and disentangled herself from Ki's arms. He looked at her, confused by her withdrawal as he watched her walk toward the rear of the house. She paused at the small hallway leading to the bedroom.

"Are you sure you want to take off your clothes to climb into that hot tub outside? We could just take off our clothes and slip into your bed, where we wouldn't have to worry about drowning."

It didn't take him more than two seconds to make his decision.

"Good idea." He managed to get the words out even as he raced across the room. He started to swing Syd up into his arms, but she stopped him just in time.

"Sorry, tiger, but I don't think you want us to have to make another trip to the emergency room," she whispered, grabbing him by his shirtfront and leading him down the hallway.

They didn't stop until the door was closed behind them and Syd was unceremoniously pushed onto the middle of the bed.

She bounced on the mattress, laughing softly as she watched the urgency of his movements while he undressed. Ki found it nerve wracking to be careful of his arm while struggling to pull his sweater over his head, and as a result, he almost ripped it off in frustration. He tossed it over his shoulder, not seeing it land on top of the dresser.

"If you don't want your clothes torn off that gorgeous body, I suggest you get them off fast." He reached for the fastener on his jeans.

Syd sat up on her knees and slapped his hands away. She tucked her hand behind the zipper as she slowly lowered the tab. When the tab could go no farther, she dipped her head and nuzzled the soft cloud of hair curled around his navel. His stomach sucked in reflexively.

"You forget something, Jones. I flirt with danger."

"Woman, the things you do to me." He knew he was reaching the point of no return. He framed her face with his hands and held it fast for a kiss that spoke of hunger, lust and something deeper, a kiss that entreated two hearts to become one. When she fell backward on the bed, he dropped with her, covering her with his body.

Their eagerness should have impeded their efforts, but they weren't going to allow anything to stop them. Ki pulled Syd's sweater over her head at the same time she was busy pushing Ki's jeans down over his hips.

"Your boots," she gasped as they both realized his jeans weren't going any farther.

Ki cursed as he sat up long enough to pull off his boots and shuck his jeans, while Syd took care of her own boots and slid her jeans down her legs.

In the dim light, Ki could make out lace-trimmed bikini panties and bra highlighting what he decided had to be the absolute best female body he'd ever seen. Syd was all lean muscle but hadn't lost her femininity. He placed his hand over her breast, finding it a perfect fit for his palm, as Syd lay back down.

"I haven't been known to be a gentle lover," he told her.

When she spoke, he could tell she was smiling by the tone of her voice. "Does that mean you won't get upset if I bite and scratch?"

If Syd was smiling, Ki was now grinning from ear to ear. What a woman!

"What did I do right to deserve a woman like you?" he murmured.

Syd wrapped her hand around his neck and pulled his face down to hers.

"Don't worry," she whispered. "I'll tend to your wounds."

Ki grasped her waist and twisted his body, rolling over onto his back until Syd lay sprawled across his body. She sat up on his hips, reaching behind her to unclasp her bra. She leisurely slid the lace-edged straps down her arms with the expertise of a striptease artist. In Ki's eyes, her disrobing was much more erotic.

"Let's be fair here. If I take off something, you should take off something." She tucked her fingers under the waistband of his briefs and tugged them downward. "My, you do know how to greet a lady, don't you, Jones?" Soft laughter gurgled in her throat.

"You still have a piece of clothing on," he pointed out.

"Not for long."

She lifted her hips enough to slide her panties down her legs.

"And now," she whispered, lowering her head as she aligned her legs with his, "let's check out that trouble we intend to get into."

Heated skin covered heated skin. Mouths mated. Words were spoken although neither would remember them later. Hot words that belied the cold temperature as Ki praised the silken feel of Syd's skin and she murmured in pleasure at the way he made her feel. They were hungry for each other and couldn't seem to get enough, no matter how much they touched each other.

Ki grasped Syd's hips and rolled them both over until he now lay on top of her.

"I want to make time stand still for us," he told her, sweeping his hands along her body, noting the lean muscle and feeling the soft skin quiver beneath his palms. "I want us to have this pocket of time where nothing else exists but us. We won't have to worry about the outside world, because it will be frozen in time."

He cupped her breasts, feeling the slight weight in his palms, the peaked nipples pressing hard. He nuzzled the soft area of skin along the side of her throat, inhaling her fragrance that was as erotic as her body. He held on to her, afraid to let go. He wasn't sure what was happening between them, but he knew neither of them would be the same again.

Syd felt the same disorientation, the same need to reach out and hold on, even as she felt the tremors within her body from his touch. She encircled him with her fingers, felt his heat and steely strength, felt the pulsing, the seeking for his other half that could only be found within her. What Ki made her feel was like nothing she'd ever felt before.

Ki wanted more than to touch Syd physically. He wanted to imprint her in every nerve in his body. He wanted to memorize her taste. He wanted all of his senses to know her. But more than that, he wanted their souls to merge until they had no idea where one began and the other ended. Ki wanted what he sensed no man ever had from Syd. He wanted her to give him everything she had hidden within herself, everything she'd never before been willing to share.

He began his seductive task with nibbles scattered along her throat. He listened to the small sounds she uttered as he made his way down across her collarbone and to the tops of her breasts. Her skin was cool at first then rapidly warmed under his lips as he nibbled and tasted the slight salt of her skin. When his mouth fastened on her nipple and suckled, her body bucked against him. He could taste the salt of her skin and couldn't imagine anything more delicious. Her body was a sinuous delight to him.

"Ki." Her voice caught as she felt the flames flicker along nerve endings wherever he touched her. She began to undulate under his grazing fingertips, rising up so the feathery touches would be intensified. He ignored her signals, her silent pleas for more, her murmured words.

"Soon," he promised, breathing softly on her ultra-sensitive skin. "Come on, Taylor, you're a spy. Didn't you ever have to endure torture?"

Syd blindly reached out, grabbing hold of his wrists, but he easily slipped them from her grasp.

Syd closed her eyes as she struggled to keep her breathing even, but she was rapidly losing the battle. A frantic part of her brain realized she had never experienced the roller-coaster effect Ki's caresses were creating. No man's mouth slid across her skin with the leisurely nonchalance his did. No man's hands had ever created such an inferno of need within her. And no man, with his wry wit and lazy smile, had ever given her the emotional pleasure he had given her. She drew in a deep breath, inhaling the sharp odor of Ki's scent that was the perfect counterpoint for her own. She gasped and blindly reached for him. "Ki, I don't think I can take much more."

His chuckle sent a waft of warm air across her damp skin. She shivered but not from the cold. "Sure you can."

Ki wondered how much longer he could last when he felt her skin melt into his and her lips move so wantonly over his body. Syd's lean body looked so delicate he couldn't help but fear he'd hurt her. The muscles quivering under his fingertips told him he had nothing to worry about. He laid his hand on her abdomen, marveling how his splayed fingers could easily reach each hip. But it was her feminine heat that coaxed him below to delve into the bright curls at the apex of her thighs. He parted the satiny petals, feeling the moisture from her arousal coating his fingers. As he dipped two fingers inside, she moaned softly. She surrounded him with a tight, moist heat that he wanted to know more intimately. He sensed, once he thrust into her, he wouldn't want to leave.

"Jones, if you don't do something very soon, I will do you a great bodily harm. You will never be able to get yourself in this situation again," she promised, curling her legs around his calves and pulling him closer against the sensuous cradle of her hips. She lowered her hand to encircle him, then trailed her fingertip down his length.

"Anything to please a lady." He fumbled with the nightstand drawer and pulled out a foil packet. Syd was determined not to make it easy as she boldly caressed him. But the moment he thrust deeply within her, she knew their lovemaking was a meeting of their souls.

As her moist heat engulfed him, drawing him in even farther, Ki knew he would never feel the same again. He wanted to take it slow and easy, but her movements were sending skyrockets shooting through his veins. When Syd looked up at him with wonder shining in her eyes as her muscles contracted around him in a tight caress, he knew there would be no holding back.

Syd was instantly transported into a world of bright lights and brilliant sounds that seemed to invade her head and travel through her body. She felt as if Ki was doing more than filling her body. He was reaching inside her head and seeing her dreams. She lifted her hips to his as she felt him thrust into her in a slow motion, but that wasn't what she wanted. She wanted the explosions. She wanted the mind-blowing experience. She wanted Ki!

"Now," she panted, feeling the quivering deep within her body.

"Wait." He grazed his teeth across her earlobe. By now his breathing was labored and his body felt so tight he wasn't sure he'd survive this.

"Now!" She felt the tremors begin and quickly escalate to major explosions.

Ki was ready to fall over the edge, too, but he wanted Syd to remember more than a night of wild sex. He wanted them to reach the stars together. "Soon."

Syd dug her nails into his hips and arched her body toward him.

While Syd was thrust upward into the bright lights, Ki felt as if he had been shot straight from a flaming volcano. Syd's cries of ecstasy were muffled by his covering mouth, and by the time they floated back to earth, neither was aware of their surroundings.

Ki slipped an arm under Syd's prone body and brought her close to him.

"Am I alive?" he wondered out loud, struggling to bring his breathing under control.

"I'm not the person to ask," she whispered, sliding her hand across his chest. Damp hair curled around her fingers. "You won't get a swelled head if I tell you that was absolutely incredible, will you?"

His laugh sounded rusty. "Honey, right now I don't think anything could swell, no matter what you say."

She lay back and stretched her arms over her head, then casually brought one arm down across Ki's middle. She smiled as she heard his breath catch and felt his muscles contract. She smiled even more widely when she slowly slid her hand downward. His sharp hiss told her he was just as surprised by his arousal.

She rolled over onto her side, propping her head on her free hand.

"Guess what, Jones. You're wrong again."

Ki rolled over onto his side to face her. "This is one time when I don't mind being wrong."

SYD'S EYES SUDDENLY flew open. When she realized it was dark, she breathed a sigh of relief. Ki lay sleeping next to her, his hand splayed possessively on her middle. She carefully inched her way toward the side of the bed.

"What?" Ki opened his eyes a slit.

"I have to go upstairs," she whispered, as if afraid the kids would overhear her. Although if they hadn't woken up a few hours ago after what had happened, she shouldn't worry now.

He looked momentarily confused. "Why?"

"I don't want the kids to wake up and find me gone." She climbed out of bed and started hunting for her clothes. She pulled her sweater over her body, then bent one knee on the bed and dropped a kiss on his lips. As if one wasn't enough, she kissed him again.

"Are you sure they won't sleep late?" he asked, grabbing hold of the front of her sweater to keep her almost where he wanted her. If he had her exactly where he wanted her, she'd be right back in bed with him.

"Are you kidding? They have built-in alarm clocks." She looked regretful at the idea of leaving him. "Will you miss me?"

He kept her sweater bunched up with his fist and lifted it up so he could press a kiss against her bare middle. "You could stay down here and I could show you how much I would miss you."

Syd muttered something about his not being fair and straightened up when he released her sweater.

"Tomorrow—today," she quickly corrected herself, "you will work on your book and we'll get out so you'll have peace and quiet to work. I'll even take the dogs with us and find a grooming parlor that will take them in for baths. I'll take the kids in to Tahoe and find Santa Claus at one of the shopping centers. I think if Heidi can see and talk to him, she'll feel as if she isn't forgotten."

It wasn't until Syd mentioned it that Ki realized that Christmas was barely a week away, although Heidi had daily restated her wish for a Talking Taffy doll. She had even gone so far as to drag Ki to the television set one day when a commercial came on showing the doll with the ten-phrase vocabulary. Heidi confided that the doll would be Barbie's new friend. Jamie only rolled his eyes and refused to talk about anything to do with Christmas, including what he might want.

"Don't worry about taking the dogs with you. They've turned out to be pretty good company when you're gone. You might have enough to worry about with Heidi. Maybe she'll need more than just seeing Santa to cheer up." He lay back among the sheets, feeling sated. But when he looked at Syd with her sweater barely covering her thighs, he began to feel more than a little aroused. He wondered if he could tempt her back into bed. He shifted enough so the sheet would slide off his body. He was pleased she looked. He only wished she would do something about it!

"I think she'll be happy as long as she can talk to Santa and believe he'll show up Christmas Eve. Hopefully, he'll explain to her he'll have no problem finding her." Syd carefully opened the door and turned to blow him a kiss. "Pleasant dreams, Jones." She slipped out, closing the door after her.

Ki lay back, straining to hear Syd's footsteps creep up the stairs but heard nothing. He pulled the pillow she'd slept on closer to him. He breathed deeply, pulling her scent into his lungs. It wasn't until he was almost asleep that something occurred to him. He started chuckling.

"I can't believe it. We forgot all about the hot tub."

Chapter Eleven

"You can't ask me for something easier?" a man's voice protested. "Why don't you ask for the list of the names and addresses of every secret service agent assigned to the White House? It would be a hell of a lot easier to latch on to than the information you're asking for."

Ki shifted his phone to his other ear. "C'm'on, Gary, you should be flattered I called you. I knew if anyone could get what I need, you could."

"Flattered, hell!"

"Be a buddy here and help me out."

"You don't understand about that agency, Ki. Information about ISA agents is more top secret than, well, anything in D.C. you can think of. I wouldn't be surprised if everything they do isn't memorized by loyal employees who had their tongues ripped out so they couldn't give away any secrets," Gary told him. "And from what I hear about the head of that department, it sounds very plausible. Leo Birch is one mean mother."

"I don't give a rat's ass about the CIA, Gary. I just want to find out about one ISA agent," he argued.

When Ki finally awoke that morning, the idea occurred to him that he might know one person who could get him information about Syd. He waited until she and the kids left before making his call.

Breakfast had proved interesting since they couldn't say anything to each other except silently. Heidi had woken up cranky and only perked up when Syd said they'd visit Santa that day, and Jamie, with eyes that were too adult for his age, looked at Syd, then at Ki, as if he knew something had gone on. Ki was just grateful that the love bite Syd had bestowed on him was in a place that was hidden by his clothing.

"Why do you want info on this Sydney Taylor?" Gary asked, breaking into Ki's thoughts.

"I've heard she's one of a kind in that sacred community. I thought an agent like her would make a good subject for a book," he lied easily.

Gary chuckled. "She'd make a great subject, but I don't think she'd talk to you. She's like all the ISA agents. Paranoid to the extreme. They keep their lives all tightly compacted in boxes that no one else can open."

Ki tensed. "It sounds as if you know her," he remarked, forcing himself to sound only mildly curious.

"I only know *of* her. I don't think anyone really knows Syd. And I know a lot of guys who think she might be a great-looking woman, but they wouldn't want to date her." He suddenly laughed. "They're

probably afraid she'd strangle them in bed or something even worse.''

Ki looked down at his hand lying on his thigh. The
fingers were tightly clenched.

''She took a leave of absence some time ago when
her brother and sister-in-law were murdered by a
crackhead trying to shake them down for money,''
Gary went on. ''Word has it, she visited the scum
while he was in jail waiting for his trial. When she left,
he was curled up on the floor crying like a baby. Right
now, she's taking care of her niece and nephew. But I
don't think it will last. Not if what all they say about
her is true. She'll get her craving for the unknown, hire
a housekeeper to look after the rug rats and take off.
She's definitely not your home-and-hearth material.
As if that's what either of us is looking for,'' he joked.

Ki's throat muscles tightened as he bit back his in-
stinctive argument. He had seen enough of Syd with
Heidi and Jamie to know she wasn't about to leave
them with anyone, no matter how trustworthy. It took
a moment for him to compose himself so he could
speak in a normal tone.

''I'm just curious to know what kind of assignments she's had and anything else you might be able
to find out about her,'' he told the man.

''Okay, but it won't be easy, and you're going to
owe me big for this one. Do you want it faxed to your
computer when I get it?'' Gary had helped Ki out with
information before and was familiar with the method.

''Yeah, but to a different number.'' He rattled off
the number. He was glad there was a phone jack in

Tripp's room. He could hook his computer up to it. "When can you get it?"

"Not as fast as the other stuff I've gotten you. I may not be able to get you anything," he warned.

"Get what you can, okay?" Ki set the phone down and returned to the computer.

Tell your readers why Baskin was so dangerous and I know you'll have a wonderful book, Syd had told him when they had a moment alone while Jamie and Heidi were upstairs.

"Easy for her to say," he muttered, staring at the blinking cursor. He was positive the words wouldn't come to him. Then another memory of Syd's leave-taking came to mind with startling clarity. Just thinking about it was enough to drive him into a state of restless energy.

Syd had come back into the cabin as Heidi and Jamie climbed into the Jeep. She grabbed Ki by the front of his shirt, pushed him behind the door and proceeded to plant the kind of probing kiss that sent his body screaming into orbit. When she stepped back, she ran her finger down his fly.

"I want you to think about this while I'm gone, big boy," she murmured, looking up at him under the sultry cover of her eyelashes. "I'm not wearing any underwear."

She sashayed away before Ki had time to come out of his stupor. He ran to the door and watched her climb into the Jeep. It wasn't until his chest started heaving that he realized he hadn't taken a breath since her provocative statement.

"No wonder men claim women will be the death of them."

"ARE YOU SURE Santa knows where we are?" Heidi asked for what Syd was convinced was the hundredth time.

"Santa knows everything," she replied.

"How?"

Syd racked her brain.

"Santa has to know," Jamie chimed in from the passenger seat. "That's why he has so many elves and helpers dressed up like him. They keep special address books for all us kids, and when we came out here, they had to know that we're out here instead of in Virginia because if they make a mistake they lose their jobs."

Heidi stared at her brother, mouth dropped open and eyes wide as she listened to his explanation.

"Really?"

He looked over the back of the seat and nodded.

"That was very good," Syd said under her breath.

He shrugged. "Dad told me the same thing when I was her age. I believed him then, so I figured Heidi would, too."

Syd blinked back the tears threatening to blind her. She reached out and gripped her nephew's hand. Instead of trying to act as if he was too big for any form of affection, Jamie curled his hand in her palm.

"There was a show about kids like us on TV one afternoon," he told her. "And a lady on there said it got easier. I miss Mom and Dad a lot, but I'm glad we have you. And I'm sorry you had to give up your job for us.''

Syd sniffed. She wasn't about to cry now. "Believe me, Jamie, my job isn't worth anything next to you guys.''

She was never so glad to see the shopping center coming up. Syd had never considered herself any good at verbalizing her emotions. Due to the danger in her work and her need to suppress her emotions for so long, she wasn't sure she knew how to express them anymore. Last night was the closest she had come to telling a man how he made her feel. From their first unorthodox meeting, Ki had fanned a flame that burned low deep within her. The thing was, what would happen when it was time for them to part? He traveled around the country writing his books. As for her... Well, Syd wasn't sure just yet what she would be doing with her life, but she had a feeling Ki didn't envision taking on a woman with two kids.

"There's Santa!" Heidi squealed, jumping up and down and pointing toward the large sign where a wooden Santa was waving his mittened hand.

Syd was glad that the little girl was still restrained in a child's safety seat. Otherwise, she probably would have bounced herself right out of the Jeep.

"And that's exactly where we're going." Syd zipped into the first parking spot she found in the crowded lot.

"We shoulda brought Ki with us," Jamie commented, jumping down to the ground.

"He has a book to write, and I don't think he's getting all that much done with us around." She zipped up Heidi's parka and adjusted her knit cap. The bright pink cap and parka intensified the color in Heidi's rosy cheeks. "Okay, Little Miss Wiggle Puss," she admonished Heidi. "You have to stick close to us."

"Don't talk to strangers or take anything from them," Heidi recited.

Syd nodded. "It's going to be real crowded in there and I don't want to lose you."

"If you do, I'm supposed to find a man wearing a uniform and tell him I'm lost."

"She'll probably talk to a pilot," Jamie said with a groan.

"A police uniform," Syd stressed, easily catching his meaning. Every day, she felt as if she was learning another facet to parenting. If she was lucky, she'd know it all by the time Heidi turned twenty-one.

Heidi's head bobbed up and down.

"Can I look at video games?" Jamie made his request.

"Yes. We'll even do some Christmas shopping," she promised.

Syd soon discovered shopping with two children meant she wasn't allowed to accomplish what she wanted to. Heidi insisted on seeing Santa and they stood in line for well over an hour along with what Syd was convinced was every child in the state.

"I could die from hunger standing here," Jamie complained.

Heidi poked him in the stomach. "I want to see Santa," she insisted. "And you're not going to stop me. I want to make sure he knows where we are."

Syd squatted down next to her. "Heidi, you can't tell Santa exactly where we're staying," she murmured.

"Why not? How else is he gonna know where we are?"

"Santa knows where we are already. Remember what Jamie told you," she said softly. "So all you have to do is remind him what you want for Christmas."

"Talking Taffy doll."

"That's right."

"'Cause Barbie needs a new friend."

"Of course."

Finally, Heidi had her picture taken with Santa. Jamie refused, on the grounds he was too old. Syd headed for the food park in the middle of the center. The children were so hungry they didn't argue for long on food choices.

"Can I get Ki a Christmas gift?" Heidi asked, chewing her way through a slice of pizza.

"Of course you can, honey." Syd was touched by her niece's idea. "Do you have anything in mind?"

Heidi stared down at the table for a moment. "He said he wished he had earplugs. Are they a nice present?"

Syd was sipping her Coke when Heidi asked her question and the liquid immediately went down the wrong way. She started choking and coughing so hard, Jamie jumped up and slapped her on the back.

"I'm sure we can find him something nice," she said between coughs.

"He still doesn't like kids," Jamie said matter-of-factly, picking up a strand of mozzarella and dropping it into his mouth. "He just tolerates us."

Syd shook her head. "No more Oprah for you, James."

"I didn't hear that on Oprah," he argued. "I was watchin' some show from Las Vegas that was like Oprah. Tomorrow they're gonna have a show about girls who married their boyfriends' dads." He made a face.

"Do me a favor. Stick with cartoons and Nickelodeon." Syd picked the rest of the mushrooms off Heidi's pizza slice and added them to her own. "We'll all be much better off."

Syd obligingly walked through the toy store, stopping long enough for Heidi to ooh and aah over the Talking Taffy doll. She watched Jamie inspect the new video games and noted she had selected ones he appeared to want the most. She asked Jamie to keep Heidi occupied while she quickly purchased a few extras for both children and even found a gift she thought would amuse Ki. When they passed a bookstore, she dragged them inside and checked out the true-crime section. After finding several of Ki's books there, she picked them up and suggested Heidi and Jamie find a couple books for themselves.

"Another stop?" Jamie groused as Syd guided them toward a pet store.

"The least we can do is bring the dogs a treat," she told him. "Then one more stop. I promise."

"Oh, sure, that's what you keep saying until you find something else."

Syd stopped in mid-stride. "James, by the time you grow up, I intend to have you acting like the closest thing to a perfect male I can. You will carry packages, you won't complain during marathon shopping sessions and you'll even learn to clean up after yourself."

He rolled his eyes. "I don't think I'm going to like it."

"No," she agreed. "But your wife will."

"Are we gonna be in here long?" Jamie groaned as he leaned against a post in the department store. They had just finished buying new parkas for Heidi and Jamie, and Syd was now looking for herself.

Heidi was sitting on the floor looking just as tired while Syd inspected racks of lingerie. She had hoped to find something interesting for Ki. She knew she might be the one wearing the item, but he would be the one appreciating it.

"I'm almost done," she assured him.

"Your poor little ones look as if they're on their last legs," a silver-haired woman cooed, stopping to pinch Jamie's cheek as she passed them. "You are quite the handsome young man, aren't you?"

Jamie opened his mouth to say something, but a warning look from his aunt stopped him.

"Thank you," he mumbled.

The woman smiled at Syd. "And so polite, too. You must be very proud of your children."

Syd smiled back. "They are unique." She pulled a semisheer black chemise off the rack.

"Can we go?" Jamie demanded.

"I'm tired," Heidi moaned, rubbing her eyes.

Syd dug out her wallet. She was glad she'd kept a charge card under a fictitious name she knew Leo couldn't trace.

"Let me pay for this and we'll be on our way."

It wasn't until Syd was herding the two tired children through the parking lot that she realized she was just as tired. But then, she realized, her weariness might have something to do with her lack of sleep the night before. Although, there had been many times when she had gone without sleep and still felt charged up the next day. She thought longingly of the hot tub and wondered if she could persuade the kids to take a nap while she relaxed in the water.

She had only driven a few miles before Heidi's body slumped down in the seat and she was sound asleep.

"Do you think I could have boots like Ki's?" Jamie asked suddenly.

Syd thought of the scarred western style boots Ki wore. "I thought you always liked athletic shoes."

"Ki's boots look more like something a guy would wear," he pointed out.

"I guess we could check out some boot shops and see if they carry your size."

"Today?"

She hated to burst his hopeful expression. "Jamie, it's getting really late. We've been gone most of the day, and I don't think we could get Heidi into another store. But I promise we'll look for some, okay?"

He shrugged. "Whatever."

"Jamie, don't be difficult, okay? I said we will go look for a pair and we will. It's not as if we haven't already done a lot today."

He turned his head and looked out the window.

Syd opted to settle for his silence. She popped a cassette in the stereo and listened to Cajun musicians playing Christmas carols on the way back to the cabin.

Once parked in the rear of the cabin, Syd tried to wake Heidi with no success and changed her tactics by asking Jamie to help carry packages inside. The boy had barely reached the back door when Ki stepped outside with the dogs behind him. They raced in circles around Syd, jumping in their excitement as they poked their noses at the packages, looking for the treats they knew their mom would bring them. Syd reached inside one bag and gave each one a rawhide chew toy. She turned back to gather Heidi into her arms.

"Here, I'll get her." Ki brushed her to one side and reached for the sleeping girl. He knew better than to suggest she was too heavy for Syd. With his luck, she'd probably challenge him to a fifty-mile run carrying hundred-pound packs. "What did you do? Slip a sleeping pill in her milk?" he asked in a low voice, sending her a heated look that reminded her of the kiss she'd given him before she left.

Obviously, he hadn't forgotten that kiss, either. She knew the memory had kept her warm all day.

"She's had a busy day between seeing Santa and drooling over Talking Taffy in the toy store," she said softly. "How was your day?"

"I accomplished more than I thought I would." He settled Heidi against his shoulder, feeling her head plop against his neck. Her mouth was open slightly and her tiny chest rose and fell with her even breathing as she unconsciously curled into a more comfortable position. "I can't believe it. She's out like a light."

Syd nodded. "She conked out not long after we left the shopping center." She grabbed hold of his sleeve to stop him. "Jamie wants a pair of boots like yours."

Ki looked down at his feet. "Really?" He had an idea he should be flattered.

"Are there any shops around that would carry some in his size?"

"No problem there. I bought a pair of great boots up here at a boot shop a few years ago and I know it's still in business. You should be able to find something there for him." He paused as if unsure how she would take his next suggestion. Heidi's weight seemed to be increasing every second, but he didn't mind. "Uh, I thought we might go look for a tree tomorrow." He rushed on. "The kids need a tree, Syd. I know you thought their getting away from familiar surroundings was a good idea for the holidays, but Heidi's worried she won't get her doll and I think Jamie's worried about something, too. Maybe if we put up a tree and decorate it, they'd feel Christmas was really coming." He looked unsure, as if he expected her to veto his suggestion.

Syd coughed to clear her throat. "That sounds like a great idea, Ki. Thank you for suggesting it."

He nodded jerkily. "There's no reason why we can't go tomorrow. There's some places around where we can cut our own tree and they'd probably get a kick out of doing that." He suddenly became aware of the sleeping girl in his arms. "I'll put her upstairs for you. Do you need any help with the packages?"

Syd shook her head. "There's nothing heavy. Jamie can help."

Ki's boots crunched on the packed snow as he walked back to the door. He stopped just before going inside. He turned around. "Hey, Syd," he called out softly so as not to awake Heidi. "Did you mean what you said this morning?"

She smiled widely. "I always mean what I say."

A strange noise erupted from his throat as he stepped inside.

"What's wrong with Ki?" Jamie asked, bounding back outside and grabbing bags from inside the rear of the Jeep. "His face was all red and he looked real funny."

Syd smiled. "I think he's glad to see us home." She promptly thought of the greeting she would give him later.

Jamie shook his head. There were days when he was positive he never wanted to be an adult. They were too confusing!

ALL THROUGH DINNER, Heidi treated Ki to a blow-by-blow account of their day.

"Santa said he could find me no matter where I was," she told him. "And when we were in the toy store, I saw a lot of Talking Taffy dolls, so I know he has one for me."

"If he doesn't she'll really scream," Jamie muttered into his applesauce.

"Thank you so much for that statement, James," Syd said dryly.

Heidi looked up at Ki. "Ki, doesn't Santa need a tree to find us?"

"He goes down a chimney, dummy, not a tree," Jamie scoffed. "Ow!" He glared at his aunt who smiled back at him innocently as if she just hadn't kicked him none too gently in the shin.

"We must really be careful so we don't hurt ourselves," she said gently.

"Actually, I thought we could look for a tree tomorrow," Ki announced.

"But Auntie Syd said we're supposed to leave you alone so you can write your book."

"I'll work after dinner for a couple of hours."

Syd forked up a piece of ham and slowly slid it into her mouth. "I've always thought I worked much better at night."

Ki almost jumped off his chair when he felt toes seem to walk up his thigh.

"Having a problem?" Syd asked, noticing his agitation.

"Nothing a cold shower couldn't cure," he muttered, praying her toes wouldn't find their way into his lap. He breathed a sigh of relief when her foot slowly wove its way down his calf.

"Can we watch *Muppet Christmas Carol?*" Heidi asked.

"They can watch anything they want to," Ki replied to Syd's inquiring expression. "I rarely watch TV outside of football season, anyway. And as I said, I'll be working on my book. I took your suggestion and detailed what the women saw when they met him and what he told me.''

She looked pleased. ''I would think with the varied subjects you write about, there are times when you look at them and wonder how you're going to portray them.''

''Auntie Syd found some of your books and bought them,'' Jamie spoke up.

''Oh, really?'' He grinned at her, gratified to see a faint red stain moving up her throat. He liked seeing her caught off guard. He doubted that happened to her too often and he was delighted to be there when it happened. ''Hey, I could have given you copies if I had known you were interested.''

''Yes, but from what I understand, writers only get paid for copies bought, and I didn't want you to be cheated out of royalties.'' She noticed the kids were finished and nodded her assent they could leave the table. She waited until she could hear the television in the other room before turning back to Ki. ''I told you before, Ki. You don't have to worry about getting a tree just for the kids.''

''Maybe it's not just for them,'' he admitted with a shrug of the shoulders. ''My mom always went all out for Christmas. The closer it gets to the holiday, the more I find myself wanting the trappings. Besides, kids need seeing a tree and stuff all around the house. Especially after the year they've gone through.''

Syd looked at Ki, suddenly realizing she was in love with the man.

Chapter Twelve

"This is absolutely decadent. And I love it!" Syd closed her eyes and emitted a soft sigh as she dropped her towel on the deck behind her and eased her naked body into the bubbling hot water. The redwood spa sat on the outside deck under a gazebo to give its occupants privacy. "Do you realize it's wintertime, there's snow on the ground all around us and we're outside sitting in a hot tub?"

Ki grinned at her as he handed her a glass filled with lime-flavored sparkling mineral water. "Only in California, Sweet Cheeks."

She shot him a droll look as she sipped her drink. "Don't call me that again, Jones, if you want to keep your bones intact," she drawled.

His grin grew wider. "I love it when you threaten me, Taylor." He set his glass down on the edge of the tub.

"You do, huh?"

"Yeah." He continued grinning, clearly enjoying his chance to taunt her. He held up his hands, his fingers wiggling in a come-hither gesture as he kept his gaze fastened on the enticing swell of her breasts visible just above the waterline. "Come on, Jane Bond, let's see what you can do."

She shook her head. "Behave, Ukiah. I'd hate for the children to hear your screams of agony when I have to torture you."

Ki nodded, acknowledging her silent suggestion that they not indulge in too much playtime out here. He wasn't disappointed. They'd be going in soon. For now, he was content to sit here and admire her. Steam rose up from the bubbling water, enveloping her in a fog. With her brightly colored hair piled on top of her head in a haphazard knot, her eyes gleaming in the dark and her skin glowing like a rare polished pearl, she had the look of an ethereal creature. Ki knew if he had a more fanciful nature, he would describe her as a creature of the woods who'd come to seduce the human male with her sensual charms.

Syd scooted down until the water covered her shoulders.

"You know, I never bothered much with shopping," she said. "A lot of the places I went to didn't have malls. Frequent traveling meant packing only the basics, since I wasn't sure how long I'd be gone and if I had to leave in a hurry I didn't want to worry about leaving a lot behind. Even now, I pack clothing that can be easily rolled up and stuffed into a duffel bag."

Ki felt pleased at the many parallels of Syd's life to his own. He really didn't have all that many personal possessions since he traveled so much and packing wasn't one of his favorite activities, either.

"Did you ever have to leave in a hurry?"

"A few times. Usually because our cover was blown." She grimaced. "I was so mad the first time it happened. I'd left behind a very expensive evening gown I'd only worn once. After that, I made sure to take clothing that I didn't mind losing." She suddenly laughed. "At one time, I had fifteen of everything in my closet. Nothing exciting."

"When you look the way you do, you don't have to worry about what you wear."

"Ah, but you forget. In my line of work, anonymity was the key."

"What are you going to do now?" He asked the question that had been haunting him for a while. He was rapidly discovering he didn't want to see Syd and the children leave the cabin. Leave him.

Syd sipped her sparkling water before she replied. "I don't have to do anything if I don't want to. Most of my money I banked, since I had no need for it. The kids were each left a trust fund that I converted into a college fund, and they have the house with me named as their trustee." Her throat muscles worked convulsively. "I guess I could always go back to school and finish getting my law degree. Or I could give a certain true-crime writer a run for his money and write about my experiences."

Ki stood up, the water running down his chest in rivulets. He made his way across the tub and sat down next to Syd. He wrapped his arms around her and pulled her against his side, sensing what she needed now was comfort, not a lover.

"Living the life of luxury isn't all that bad, you know," he murmured. "You could always hire your-

self some stud for your housekeeper. Maybe somebody with more muscles than you have. Somebody
named Dirk or Rex or..." He tried to come up with
another appropriate name. "Well, you know what I
mean."

Syd's shoulders started shaking. Not with tears as
Ki first feared, but with laughter.

"Dirk or Rex?" she said with a gasp. "That last one
sounds more like an Irish setter than a male housekeeper."

He was unfazed by her comment. "You could get
one of those, too. I guess the kids wouldn't mind having another dog. They'd need someone to play with
while you're playing with Rex."

Syd laughed. "That is so bad."

"You're right, an Irish setter would probably try to
eat Cocoa and Bogie. Maybe something smaller," he
went on.

Syd shook her head against the curve of his shoulder. Flyaway strands of her hair caressed his face and
he imagined he could smell the scent of her shampoo.
Ki quickly realized he wanted more than just to comfort her.

"Sydney," he said in a husky voice, using his hands
to raise her face to his. "Ever make love in a hot tub?"

She placed one hand against his chest. "No."

"Ever make love with a famous writer?"

"Yes."

His brows drew together as he absorbed her answer. "Who?"

Her lips feathered across his jaw until they reached
the corner of his lips.

"You."

He snaked an arm around her rear end and lifted her onto his lap. Syd curled her arms around his neck and leaned back. "Are you sure no one can see us?"

"We guys came out here a lot and didn't worry about being seen."

She placed her fingertips against his lips. As she moved closer, she could feel his arousal against her, teasing her each time she brushed against him.

"That's not exactly the same."

"True, we tended to get involved in belching contests. Guy stuff." He stroked the sides of her breasts, his fingertips barely touching her where she wanted to be touched.

Syd was never shy and she proved it now. She leaned forward, taking his mouth in a hungry kiss that spoke of her yearnings for him all day while she was away from him. She caressed him with that same hunger, fueling a fire in Ki that flared into an inferno.

"I'm selfish, Ki," she whispered, pressing fierce kisses along the hard line of his jaw. "I want more of you than you can imagine ever giving any other woman." She stared down into his dark green eyes. "I've decided I want it all."

As he listened to her rawly spoken words, his hands against her sides tightened their hold. There would probably be bruises on her skin by morning, but at the moment it didn't matter. There was so much need between them that they couldn't find words to describe their feelings. They allowed their hands and lips to communicate for them.

Ki grasped Syd's hips, lifting her up slightly and slowly lowering her onto him. Her eyes widened slightly then softened with emotion as she tightened her muscles around his hardness, pulling him in ever deeper in a tight silken glove. She kneeled on either side of Ki, moving her hips in a slow rotating movement.

"We're crazy to do this out here," she whispered against his mouth. She flicked her tongue across his bottom lip then slipped inside to drink from him. At first, he tasted cool and tart from the lime-flavored drink, but his lips warmed rapidly as their kisses grew more feverish. They barely came up for air, as if they needed none as long as they could sustain each other.

"We're not crazy," he told her, starting to feel the tension twist deep down inside as she surrounded him.

She flexed her muscles and tightened them each time he thrust upward. She wanted it to last forever. But it wasn't to be. She felt the tiny tremors deep inside first. A warning that they couldn't be together much longer.

Ki felt as if Syd's body had been specially made for him. As if her skin had been fashioned from the finest silk and her hair from strands woven by woodland fairies. He knew his thoughts were fanciful, but there was something about her that brought that side of him out.

He adored her upper body, the skin glistening with droplets of water that streamed down her chest only to be caught by the aroused tips of her nipples where they shone like iridescent diamonds on her skin. He suddenly wanted to see her covered in diamonds and pearls, so that she could shimmer like a beacon in the night. A beacon only he would follow.

He felt the tension increase as her body clenched as if unwilling to release him. His thrusts increased in fervor as he raced for that summit, holding on to her tightly. He felt himself erupt and felt her own frantic movements against him, and he knew they had crossed into a whole new territory of emotion.

Ki was first stirred into consciousness by the feel of warm moisture against his face. He tipped his head back enough to look down at the face so close to his own. Syd's cheeks were damp with water droplets that shone silver in the night. He pressed one of his fingers against a droplet and brought it to his lips. The salty taste confirmed his suspicions.

"Syd." He gently raised her chin. "Why are you crying?"

She shook her head, sniffing audibly. "I never..." She took a deep breath to compose herself. "I thought before it was special, but just now..." She again shook her head, unable to come up with the right words. Instead, her tears kept flowing.

Ki was stunned. He knew Syd wasn't the type to easily cry and this unnerved him. When he realized she wasn't going to stop, he gathered her up in his arms, grabbed their towels, wrapping one around her shoulders, and made a hasty retreat for the door.

He carried her into the bedroom and set her on the bed. He went into his bathroom and grabbed another towel.

"Syd, do you want a handkerchief or anything?" he asked, crouching down in front of her.

She swiped her face with one hand as she shook her head.

Ki dried her off as carefully as if she were fashioned of rare porcelain. He even carefully searched for the clip that held her hair on top of her head and released it.

"I can't stop crying," she whispered, looking as mournful as a small child.

Syd, who was so used to controlling her emotions, was stunned by her inability to stop.

Since he didn't have a robe to his name, Ki settled for draping one of his flannel shirts around her, pushing her arms in the sleeves and buttoning it up. As if fearing that wasn't enough, he reached behind her, pulling back the covers, and urged her toward the pillows.

Syd crawled to the center of the bed, then moved over when Ki joined her. They huddled together under the covers.

"Maybe it's overload from all the tension you've put on yourself," he said, looking for an explanation.

"My body isn't allowed to overload."

"Maybe so, but there's always a first time."

Syd curled up against Ki's side. With her arms wrapped around his middle, she felt as if her tears would finally stop. Deep down, she sensed her emotional well-being turning upside down. And it all had to do with Ki.

She hadn't had many lovers. One, because of her work. Two, because she didn't believe in sex for physical nourishment. The few lovers she'd had in the past had always become good friends. But none had reached deep inside her soul the way Ki had.

Here she was, no longer a gun-toting government agent with the world at her feet. Now she was an out-of-work government agent with two children looking to her for their safety. And the man who fascinated her most was definitely not a father figure. His work required he travel just as she had once traveled. With two school-age children, it wouldn't be possible for her to join him.

Syd didn't resent Jamie and Heidi. The moment she heard Shane and Jenny were gone, she didn't hesitate in taking a leave of absence so she could be with the children. And once with them, she realized, in some ways, she needed them more than they needed her. It didn't take long for her to come to the decision to leave the agency. She knew she couldn't be the parent Shane and Jenny would have been for them, but she would make sure they had the best childhood she could give them. Besides, if she was honest with herself, she had to admit all the travel and the constant looking over her shoulder was getting to be too much. She wondered if that meant her biological clock was ticking overtime.

Speaking of biological clocks... A part of her wouldn't mind if Ki stopped by to visit every so often. But it wasn't what she wanted to think about now. Not when he held her in his arms as if she was the only thing he cared about.

"Maybe it's pre-Christmas blues," she murmured, burying her face against the curve of his shoulder. She inhaled the sharp scent of his skin. Usually he smelled of a spicy soap and an after-shave that echoed that same spice aroma. Right now, he smelled of her, just as she knew she carried his scent on her skin. "Or post-Christmas shopping fatigue. You haven't lived until you've spent the day in a shopping mall with two young children. I had no idea how many video games were available until Jamie pointed each one out. Each one he didn't have, that is. And Heidi learned that Talking Taffy will have a baby brother coming out soon." She shuddered. "She's already talking about the brother for her birthday."

"When's her birthday?" Ki asked, not seeing anything wrong with that.

"September."

"Good ole Taffy might have a whole family by then."

"I wouldn't be surprised." Syd looked up at him. A part of her wanted to ask him what would happen with them. Was there more to them than great sex? She felt there was and hadn't been adverse to voicing her questions in the past. So why was she nervous about doing it now?

There could only be one reason. She was afraid his answer might not be the one she wanted to hear.

Desperate for that closeness again, Syd rolled over on top of Ki.

"Tell you what, handsome," she murmured against his lips, then sat up in his lap and began unbuttoning his shirt. "This time I promise not to cry."

When Syd left Ki's bed in the early morning hours, he lay there awake, listening to her soft footsteps upstairs. As he scooted farther down the bed, his foot encountered something.

"What the—?" he reached down and pulled out a rawhide lollipop. The one Syd had given Bogie that afternoon. "I thought she was kidding when she said he hid his treats." He chuckled and tossed it onto the nightstand.

As he lay back, Ki thought about the quiet time he was going to have here. Little did he expect when he came up here to finish his book that he'd be bombarded by a woman, two kids and two dogs—and that he'd love it. Not only did he love the situation, but he had a good idea he was falling in love with the woman, too.

"Oh, Tripp, I just bet you'd be laughing your ass off if you could see what I've gotten myself into."

"How DO WE KNOW what tree we can have?" Heidi looked down the row of trees.

"We can choose any tree that doesn't have a red tag on it," Ki explained.

At his suggestion, they had come out to the Christmas tree farm right after breakfast. Ki had hoped all the good trees wouldn't be chosen, even though it was getting close to the twenty-fifth, but he hadn't expected to see so many red tags hanging from trees, either.

"We have to have a big one," the little girl pronounced, looking at one tagged tree with a forlorn gaze. In deference to the season, Syd had dressed her in bright green wool pants and the green-and-white parka with matching wool cap and mittens she'd bought at the mall the day they went shopping. Heidi giggled when Ki told her she looked like one of Santa's elves. "We had a big tree last year."

"You were too little to remember Christmas last year!" Jamie scoffed. "And we didn't have a big tree, either."

Her tiny chin stuck out as she glared at her brother. "Did so."

"It was a nice Christmas and that's all you need to remember." Syd stepped in. "Why don't we concentrate on looking for a tree? And not a big one. We're going to have to buy lights and ornaments as it is."

"So Santa can find us."

"She's gonna want a really big tree." Jamie looked as bored as a nine-year-old could.

"Don't worry, Jamie, we'll find something in between," Ki assured him. He started to walk off then turned around. He held out his hand to Syd. With a smile that he could have sworn was shy, she tucked her hand inside of his and followed along.

As Heidi and Jamie argued the merits of various trees, Ki was content to walk with Syd's hand clasped in his and draw the clean, sharp scent of pine-scented air deep into his lungs.

"It's such a beautiful day," she commented, raising her face to the blue sky. Her skin seemed to glow from the sun that shone down on the snow-dappled ground. Voices of others looking for that special tree were muted by the rows of pines. Occasionally, the squeal of a child echoed in the air. "This is the kind of day a person should be outside to enjoy."

He ducked his head and nuzzled her neck. "Only if you're with the right person."

The sultry look she sent him under the cover of her lashes was hot enough to melt the snow around them. "Careful, sir, you might embarrass me."

Ki released her hand long enough to sneak a pinch to her bottom. He laughed when she yelped in outrage and grabbed her hand again. He only wished they weren't wearing gloves so he could feel her skin against his. Ki had discovered from the first moment he touched her that there was nothing like the feel of Syd's skin. He wasn't sure what she put on it, but to him, it always felt like silk and smelled like heaven. He raised her hand and pressed a kiss against the inside of her wrist. As his lips lingered on the blue-tinged veins, he could feel the tempo of her pulse increase and her scent release with the warmth.

"I guess that will have to hold me until later," he murmured, shooting her a look that spoke volumes.

"I want today to last forever," she told him.

"You want everything to last forever."

Syd looked around to make sure Heidi and Jamie were still in view. Once she was assured they were, she turned back to Ki. "You once said you wanted time to stand still. For us to create our own pocket of time. This is our pocket of time." She held her free arm out, gesturing to the trees around them.

Ki looked down at her upturned face. She wore little makeup other than a touch of bright coral lip gloss. Her cheeks were already flushed from the cold air, and dark mascara highlighted her eyes in a way no eye shadow could. She had traded her dull navy wool cap for a bright red one with a red-and-white tassel that reminded him of a candy cane. She told him she bought it because of the bright color that she felt she needed after living so long in dark shadows. The color should have clashed with her hair but managed not to. She had pulled it back in a French braid, but tiny wisps managed to escape to curl around her face. As she smiled up at him and her eyes danced with laughter, he swore she looked as young as Heidi and Jamie. He reached out, tucking a stray hair behind her ear. His hand lingered against her cheek. He had no idea just how open his expression was as he gazed down at her.

"We found one!"

It took a moment for Heidi's excited announcement to penetrate their absorption with each other.

"I guess we should see if they were able to compromise on a suitable size," Syd murmured.

"Either way, it's got to fit in the truck," he warned, taking her hand and walking rapidly in the direction of Heidi and Jamie, who were jumping up and down in their excitement.

"It doesn't have a red tag," Jamie shouted.

"And it's real bushy," Heidi added.

"It's perfect," Syd pronounced.

"And . . ." Ki drew the word out.

"It's big." Syd had to tip her head backward in order to see the tree's top.

"Very big," Ki agreed. "Heidi, it can't fit in the Jeep."

"Sure it can. All the people put the tree on top of their cars," she explained. "Why can't we do that?"

Syd winced at the vision of scratches marring the top of her Jeep.

He crouched down in front of the little girl. "The Jeep isn't long enough, honey."

"But your truck is bigger. Why didn't we bring that?"

"Because there aren't enough seats in it for you and Jamie," he explained patiently.

She looked at him with eyes the same vivid color as Syd's. "But we could come back for it with your truck, right?"

"Yeah, your truck is bigger," Jamie chimed in. Clearly, he wanted the tree as much as Heidi did.

"Let's see you come up with a good answer now," Syd said under her breath.

"Heidi, you're going to grow up to be a great lawyer," Ki told her. He looked up at Syd. "Shall we get one of those red tags? Jamie and I can come back later today."

She looked up at the towering tree again. "Do you realize how many lights and ornaments that will take? Not to mention whether you can get it inside the cabin without chopping off several feet?"

He shrugged. "Hey, you're only five and nine once. We'll find a way." He snaked his arm around Heidi's waist and hoisted her up. She laughed merrily and twined her arms around his neck in a stranglehold as he added their red tag to the slip already attached to one of the branches.

"I love you, Ki," Heidi told him, planting a cold kiss on his cheek.

He grinned, warmed inside by her unfettered affection. "And I love you, little elf." He looked down at Syd. *But the one I love most is you, Taylor. Now all I have to do is get up the nerve to tell you so. Without compromising my bachelor status.*

Chapter Thirteen

After spending a couple hours combing stores for enough lights and ornaments to cover the tree, they stopped for hamburgers.

Once they entered the fast-food restaurant, Ki suggested the others find a table while he ordered their food.

"So what does everyone want?"

Syd held up her hand as Jamie and Heidi began talking at the same time.

"No, I'm not letting him get caught in the trap I got caught in," Syd told them. She looked up at Ki. "Heidi will have the Tiny Tots Meal with an orange soda for her drink and ask that her hamburger be made up plain. She doesn't even want cheese on it. No pickles on Jamie's cheeseburger. He doesn't want them to even touch the meat and he can handle a medium Coke." She smiled at her nephew. "They can share the fries that come with Heidi's meal. I'll have a cheeseburger with everything on it, large order of fries and a large Coke. Got that?"

Ki's eyes glazed over. "I hope so."

"I'll help." Jamie jumped off his seat and happily followed Ki to the order counter.

"Auntie Syd, can we keep Ki?" Heidi pulled four paper napkins from the dispenser and carefully placed one where each of them would sit.

Something twisted deep within Syd. "Honey, he's not a puppy. We're staying in his cabin now, but pretty soon we'll have to go back home because Jamie has school."

"And I get to go to school soon 'cause I'm five now."

She smiled and nodded. "Yes, you will."

Heidi looked over her shoulder where Ki and Jamie were standing at the counter. Syd noticed that Ki was speaking to the girl taking the orders while Jamie stood beside him trying to imitate Ki's natural loose-hipped slouch.

"But Ki doesn't have anybody like you have us," she told Syd. "If we kept him, he'd have all of us. He likes us more than he used to. I can tell. He doesn't make nasty faces at us like he did and he doesn't say bad words all the time. I think he would be better off with us," she stated.

Syd smiled. She reached across the table and used her fingers to brush the little girl's feathery bangs to one side. Not because they needed it, but because she felt the need to touch her. As she looked in Heidi's face, she saw her own features stamped in miniature. Even the slight bow of the upper lip was identical to hers. The little girl was already showing Syd's inherent tendency to jump before thinking. Syd only hoped

Heidi would learn to temper that part of her personality, as she had, before it was too late.

"Ki has a life of his own," she reminded her. "But I don't see any harm in our borrowing him for a while."

"Okay, we have a Tiny Tots Meal with an absolutely naked hamburger and a small orange soda." Ki began unloading his tray. "Jamie made sure no pickle dared come near his cheeseburger, and here's your cheeseburger with everything on it and large fries." He placed Syd's meal in front of her.

"If you ever get stuck with your writing, you'd make a terrific waiter," she told him, smiling her thanks.

He bumped her with his hip as he slid onto the bench seat beside her. "Nah, too much work."

Syd stuck a straw in the top of Heidi's cup and divided the fries between the two kids.

Ki looked around the colorful restaurant. The Christmas music was loud to compensate for the noise from the younger clientele and the decor was well on the brash side. Then he looked at Syd who was as colorful as her surroundings.

"If anyone had told me I'd ever be sitting in a fast-food restaurant with a beautiful woman and two kids I'd suggest they seek professional help," he told her under the cover of the kids' chattering to each other. "If I'm not careful, my whole reputation could be destroyed."

Syd's smile froze on her lips as she thought that maybe Ki hadn't changed as much as they thought he had. "I don't think you have too much to worry about."

SYD AND HEIDI OPENED boxes of tree lights and ornaments while Ki and Jamie left again to pick up the tree. Syd had finished unraveling the strings of lights and testing them to make sure all the bulbs lit up when Ki's truck appeared at the top of the road.

"Look!" Heidi squealed, jumping up and down, clapping her hands with glee.

"This tree is not for you guys," Syd told the dogs who stood beside her as she watched Ki and Jamie hop out of the truck. Ki began loosening the ropes that had secured the tree to the top of the truck. There were black smudges on his sweatshirt and another smudge on his cheek.

Heidi looked up. "Why not? Cocoa and Bogie love trees."

"They can only play around outdoor trees, not indoor ones," she explained, opening the door and stepping outside. "It looks taller than it did at the tree farm."

"Just be glad you weren't the one cutting it down," Ki puffed, maneuvering the tree onto the ground. "The guy assured me this heavy-duty stand would easily hold it. If it doesn't, we could be in a lot of trouble."

"It took Ki and three other guys to put the tree on the truck. They all cussed," Jamie said helpfully.

Syd patted his shoulder. "I wouldn't worry. It was probably for a good cause. I checked the lights for you," she told Ki. "We're in luck. They all worked beautifully. We also cleared a corner for the tree.'' She looked at it with a critical eye. "I hope we cleared enough room for it. It looks awfully big.''

"Thanks." He scowled at the large tree trunk as he tried to shift it into the large metal stand. "Out of here, dog. This tree would flatten you into a pancake." He used his foot to gently push Bogie away. He was instantly overbalanced by the heavy tree. "I need help here!''

Syd jumped to grab the other side before Ki and the tree toppled to the ground.

"I really hate to ask this, but will you be able to get the tree inside the cabin without any problems?''

"*We.* We will get it into the cabin," he told her, crouching down so he could tighten the screws that dug into the base of the trunk. He looked up from his task. "You couldn't have tried to talk her into a smaller tree, could you?''

"Heidi's like me. She can't be easily swayed," she said without apology, still holding on to the trunk. She resisted the urge to release one hand to scratch at the itching sensation that was traveling up her arm. A wave of nostalgia came over her, and memories surfaced of her father wrestling with their Christmas tree as he worked to get it to fit in a tree stand. "Shouldn't you put it in the stand after you get it in the house?''

He glanced up with a look that bordered on extreme frustration. "You've never had a live tree, have you?''

"Not since..." She had to think a moment. "It's been a long time."

"Then do me a favor and just stand there holding the damn tree while I get it in the stand *outside* before I take it *inside,* just in case I have to cut off any lower branches."

She shrugged, unable to comprehend his frustration.

"This is going to be great. Just think of it," she said softly. "All the lights off except those on the tree. Maybe a fire burning. Soft music on the stereo." She paused until Ki looked up. "And me. What more could a man want?"

"A good stiff drink. Hey! Dammit, Syd!" His scowl was no match for her look of pure innocence. "Don't let go of that again."

It took a lot of huffing and puffing on Ki's part, directions from Syd, and Heidi and Jamie keeping the dogs out of the way, but eventually the tree was set in the corner Syd and Heidi had decided on. Syd helped move the stereo equipment over another eighteen inches.

"The rest is up to you." Ki sighed and dropped onto the couch. He scratched his forearm and pulled fir needles off his sweatshirt. "I'm too old for this. No wonder Mom has one of those little artificial trees. This is too much work!"

Syd stared at the tree as if afraid it would suddenly list to one side.

"I'll get you something to drink," she offered, patting his shoulder on her way to the kitchen.

As Syd passed Ki's bedroom, the phone rang once then suddenly stopped. She stopped in the bedroom doorway when she heard several high-pitched tones. It wasn't until then she realized that his computer modem was receiving information.

"One of your admirers is calling you," she teased. "I hope your computer has enough memory to handle it all."

She barely had the words out of her mouth when Ki skidded to a stop in front of her.

"Good, I was waiting for that," he said. "It's stuff about a book I'm thinking of doing after I finish this one. Tell you what, don't worry about anything to drink for me right now." He went into his room and, for the first time in days, closed the door.

Syd stared at the door, stunned by Ki's abrupt change in personality. And feeling that twinge deep down that usually warned her something was not right. The last time she had that feeling, she narrowly escaped with her life. She imagined she could hear the steady hum of his laptop, although she knew the sound was only in her mind. She dreaded to think what danger his new project might be putting him in.

"Ki, what are you doing?" she whispered before she turned away.

KI SAT ON THE BED, hitting the down arrow in steady progression as he read first the note Gary sent him, containing a warning to delete the information as soon as possible. He quickly scrolled downward. And what he read chilled him to the bone.

He ignored the rest of the fir needles still stuck to his sweatshirt and his itchy skin in desperate need of a hot shower. The information scrolling down the screen was too interesting to leave. And damn scary.

"Syd, what have you been doing all these years?" he murmured in horrified fascination as he scrolled from one assignment to another. What started out as what would be considered relatively easy assignments for a rookie agent soon escalated. He now understood a lot of things about her.

Syd's admission was true. She *was* a danger junkie. The more difficult and dangerous the assignment, the more she excelled. He learned she could slip in and out of situations and identities as easily as a chameleon. Many agents had their strengths in certain areas. Syd's seemed to be in the weapons' area. She was conversant with every military weapon available and had the ability to use most of them. She also was considered a valuable ally for many of the major arms dealers in the world. In the time she had dealt with many of them, her cover had been blown only a few times. Anyone who discovered her identity was no longer living. And she was able to return to her own life because it was kept so far from the one she lived.

Ki felt a bone-numbing cold seep into his veins. When he had requested information about Syd, he had expected it to be routine: her personal life, perhaps a few reports about her past assignments. He hadn't expected anything this complete.

He scanned reports Syd had written after her assignments. He even looked through personal reports about Syd that included intimate details Ki had no desire to know. The more he read, the sicker he got.

Before he switched off the computer, he had the good sense to hide the file under a false name. He trusted Syd not to snoop, but he decided it wouldn't hurt to be a little paranoid. Just in case.

Ki headed for the shower. He hoped he could wash away the memories along with the dirt. He already sensed it wouldn't be all that easy.

SYD FELT KI'S ABSENCE, as he didn't come out for the rest of the afternoon and had to be called several times for dinner. When he emerged, he was quiet and didn't look at her.

"I made a quick trip into town while you were working and picked up a pizza," she said.

"You have to see the tree." Heidi pulled on his hand as she led him into the combination living-family room. "Doesn't it look pretty? Except Bogie kept trying to eat the ornaments and Cocoa played with some of them. Auntie Syd turned on the lights. See, isn't it pretty?"

Ki stopped short at the fairy-tale sight before him. He thought of the back-breaking trouble of hoisting the tree onto the truck. The rough bark that abraded his palms. The tree almost falling on him. All of that didn't matter now.

Syd had taken a white sheet and draped it under the tree to add to the illusion. Tiny, bright, colored lights twinkled among the dark green branches. Twirling glass balls reflected the lights. The silver foil icicles were clumped unevenly in places, probably due to Heidi's enthusiastic assistance, but it didn't matter. The magic was there.

"I found a stepladder in the kitchen and used it to reach the top branches," Syd said with great satisfaction as she came up to stand behind him. "It turned out even better than I thought it would." She ran her fingers lightly down his spine. "So, now we have the tree and the lights. We just need the soft music and me."

Ki found he couldn't get into the spirit. He managed a smile that was only a ghost of his usual one. He turned away without any comment or reaction to her teasing caress.

"Yeah."

Syd's gaze was a troubled one as she watched him return to his room.

"Ki, are you having trouble with your book?" she asked, just before he stepped inside.

"Yeah, I am," he said quietly. "Don't expect to see me for the rest of the evening. I'm going to see if I can iron things out."

"All right."

Syd watched him close the door behind him with a quiet click that seemed to signify so much. She felt an uneasy lump in the pit of her stomach. His hesitation before he answered had been so slight that most wouldn't have noticed it. But Syd was well trained and easily noticed even the slightest inaccuracies in human behavior. Something was bothering him, all right. But it wasn't his book.

"THE TREE IS SO PERFECT, Auntie Syd," Heidi told her as she crawled under the covers later that evening.

After dinner, Syd had kept them occupied playing games until it was time for baths and their bedtime. "With our tree, Santa can find us real easy."

"I didn't think he'd have had any trouble finding us before," Jamie muttered, glancing at Syd as he slid under his own covers.

As Syd looked at their faces, she realized the dark shadows had disappeared from under their eyes and the strain had left their faces. Heidi hadn't woken up in the middle of the night with bad dreams for quite a while and Jamie also slept much better. She could see them turning back into the exuberant kids she remembered before Shane's and Jenny's death. The ones she had prayed so hard to see again.

She gathered Heidi up in a bone-crunching hug. She could smell the mingled scents of shampoo and the raspberry soap Heidi insisted on using in her bath since it had been her mother's favorite.

"I promise you the best Christmas I can give you," she whispered, kissing her cheek.

"We'll have a good Christmas," Heidi insisted, confused by her statement. "Jamie 'n' me will have you and Ki with us. That will make it really good."

"Except I don't think Ki likes us anymore."

Syd's head shot up at Jamie's statement. She had no idea he had noticed the same thing she had.

"Why do you say that, Jamie?"

"He didn't talk during dinner and he looked at you funny. Almost like he did when we first got here. Does he know you're a spy?"

Syd nodded. "I told him, but he'll keep our secret."

"And he'll keep Mean Mr. Leo away, too," Heidi decided, having already chosen Ki as her new hero.

"You know what?" Syd tapped her forefinger against Heidi's nose. "I don't think we need to worry about Mean Mr. Leo anymore." She adjusted Heidi's covers, then made a show of tucking Jamie in although he always insisted he was too old to be tucked in.

Syd changed into a nightgown and robe before she returned downstairs. On her way into the kitchen, she peeked toward Ki's room. The door was still closed. It remained closed as she curled up on the couch reading a book. When she put it down, she couldn't remember one word she'd read. She finally gave up and went back upstairs.

She lay in bed with a dog on each side of her to keep her warm. It wasn't the same as Ki's arms around her. And as she lay awake, she still couldn't escape the uneasy feeling that refused to go away.

Chapter Fourteen

"What are you doing this far out in my neck of the woods, boy?"

Ki looked up as the rough voice rang out. Zeke suddenly appeared between two trees. With a rifle cradled in his arms, wearing ancient army fatigues and laced-up combat boots, he looked like the eccentric hermit he was.

"Sorry if I'm getting too close to your still, Zeke."

The grizzled old man scowled at him. "What still? I don't have no still, Ki Jones, and you know it. They're against the law."

Ki smiled at the blatant lie. "Don't worry. I won't give your secret away. I needed to get out and thought a hike would do me some good. I guess I sort of wandered out this way."

He needed to do something to sort out his feelings of the past few days. He already knew he was acting like a bastard to Syd, but he wasn't sure how to fix it without confronting her with what he knew. And he wasn't ready to do that just yet. So, instead, he talked *at* Syd instead of *to* her.

And he saw the hurt turning her eyes a dull color as she looked at him with questions he wasn't ready to answer. Probably because he had a lot of questions of his own he wanted answered. She wasn't going to be happy when she found out he knew what he did about her. So he turned himself inward while he tried to figure things out for himself. Maybe then he could come to terms with his feelings for Syd. Because how do you love a government agent—even an ex-government agent—whose middle name was danger?

She'd teased him about danger in their relationship many times, but now that he knew what he did, he realized that was nothing compared to the danger she encountered in her work. And it made his blood turn cold at the idea she could have been shot and left bleeding in some foreign country and no one probably would have given a damn about her! Funny that the guy who would end up caring was the same one who vowed there would never be one special woman in his life.

Zeke lifted his face skyward. "Not a good day for a walk. I wouldn't be surprised if we got more snow by nightfall. You should be back in that cabin with that little lady of yours. She'd be a hell of a lot prettier to look at than this old face. And a hell of a lot warmer."

"Yeah, I know."

The older man stared at Ki long and hard. As if he'd come to a decision, he looked around to make sure no one else was lurking around. He curved his arm over his head and gestured.

"Come on, I'll get ya somethin' to warm ya up."

Ki shuddered at the thought of Zeke's idea of a warm-up drink. He'd be lucky to have any stomach lining left.

"If you don't mind, I'd like to live out the rest of this year, Zeke," he said, following the man.

He snorted his contempt. "You kids today can't take the good stuff. You'd be a hell of a lot better off with my brew than those fancy wine coolers everybody drinks. They're nothin' more'n colored water, boy. You might as well drink milk as drink that."

"I never turn down beer." But he wouldn't turn down a chance to sit with Zeke and momentarily forget about his worries. Who could tell? Maybe Zeke's paint thinner that doubled for a drink would have his answers for him.

"Beer's for sissies," Zeke scoffed, ambling off with Ki on his heels. "We're gettin' us a man's drink. Then you can tell me what's got you so bothered."

"If you can come up with an answer," Ki muttered, "you're a hell of a better man than I am."

"Okay, we've got it all. A snow dad, snow mom, snow girl, snow boy and a snow dog." Syd stood back and examined their handiwork. "It is a snow dog, isn't it?"

After Ki had taken off that morning without a word as to where he was going, Syd asked the kids if they wanted to build a snow family in the front yard of the cabin. They quickly said yes and bundled up against the cold. Syd slipped sweaters on the two dogs before they all ventured outdoors.

The day was crisp and very cold, a perfect day, she explained, for constructing their snow family. It took them all morning, and after a break for lunch, they had returned to their tasks. They had finished the last statue only a few moments before.

Jamie stood in front of her, also studying the figures. "It looks more like a rat to me. You shouldn't have let Heidi make the dog. She doesn't do it very well."

Heidi stamped her foot. "Don't you make fun of my dog! He looks just like Cocoa and Bogie."

"How can it when it doesn't even look like a dog?"

"All right, Jamie. Heidi, it's a wonderful dog." Syd stepped in to mediate. "How about some hot chocolate to celebrate? We've been out here so long I'm surprised we haven't turned into snow people ourselves."

"Can we have a snowball fight afterward?" Jamie asked.

"Maybe tomorrow."

"Hey, there!"

Syd and the children turned at the sound of Ki's voice. Syd hoped she was the only one who noticed Ki was walking a little awkwardly.

"Did you have a nice walk?" Her voice was as chilly as the air.

"Just great." He seemed to be working hard at enunciating his words. "I ran into Zeke. He invited me back to his place and we talked for a while. Or I should say he talked. He likes to relive his days during World War II." He walked up to Syd and crooked his arm around her neck, pulling her close for a kiss.

She thought she'd choke from the fumes. "I'd say you did a lot more than talk." She wrinkled her nose. "I'd tell you what you smell like, but I'm not sure if it's turpentine or worse."

"It was real cold, so we had a little something." He held up his thumb and forefinger extended a fraction apart. He noticed the figures at the edge of the yard. "What do we have here?"

"We've been playing in the snow this morning," Syd told him. "There's a snow dad, snow mom, snow boy, snow girl and snow dog."

Jamie suddenly giggled. He pointed toward the figures. "Look."

Heidi looked over and suddenly screamed. "No, Cocoa, Bogie, no!"

Jamie bent over laughing so hard he couldn't talk as the dogs angled alongside the snow dog and each lifted a rear leg.

"I guess they didn't like Heidi's snow dog." Syd pressed her lips together to keep from laughing.

Ki coughed to hide his laugh.

"Bad dogs! Bad!" Heidi shrieked, running after them.

The two dogs scampered off, looking confused by her anger. To them, it was nothing more than a white tree.

"Come on, let's get some hot chocolate." Syd herded them inside. "And hot coffee for you," she muttered to Ki.

"Why? I'm nice and toasty."

"Toasty isn't the word I'd use."

Syd set cups of water in the microwave for the kids'
hot chocolate and poured coffee for herself and Ki.
She placed a plate of cookies on the table to complete
their snack.

She waited until the children finished their hot
chocolate and ran upstairs to play.

"What is wrong with you?" she asked bluntly.

Ki looked her square in the eye. Syd had made the
coffee strong enough to float the entire Seventh Fleet.
"Nothing."

"I don't believe you."

He got up and poured himself another cup.
"Sometimes I think Zeke's home brew could strip
paint," he commented, as if the tension between them
hadn't grown to the breaking point. He sat down and
picked up a cookie. "It looks like you three were busy
this morning. This must be a change from your usual
way of killing time." There was a bite in his words Syd
hadn't heard from him in a long time.

She reached across him with lightning speed and
grasped his wrist, gently pressing her thumb on a nerve
that she knew would produce a tingling sensation
along his arm. If she pressed harder, he would lose all
feeling for a while. She was tempted to press another
nerve that would render him unconscious. Maybe
when he came to, he'd have the answers she wanted.

As if he hadn't noticed a thing, Ki slowly turned his
head.

"Don't even think about it." The warning was given
in a flat voice that was more unsettling than any anger he might have exhibited.

Syd reared back, surprised by his vehemence. She stared at him, stunned. The man seated across from her wasn't the same man who made such wild wonderful love to her. The man who held her in his arms offering sweet comfort. The man she was in love with.

Ki broke the eye contact first. He stood up and carried his cup to the sink. He walked out of the kitchen without looking at her.

"I think I'll take a hot bath. It's been a long day."

"Ki."

He wouldn't have turned, but there was a slight catch in her voice that tugged at his soul.

"Don't do this." Syd broke all her rules by begging, but by now she didn't care. "Not to us."

"I have some things I need to work out in my mind," he said quietly. "We'll talk later."

"Will we?" The softly spoken words followed him into his room.

Ki collapsed against his door. He was queasy from Zeke's home brew and tired from all the walking he'd done that day. He stared at his computer as if it would hold all the answers. One did come to him. What he did was wrong. He'd basically investigated her instead of waiting for her to tell him. As he pushed away from the door, he came to the decision of going in and deleting Syd's file after his bath. And he'd make damn sure she never found out what he'd done.

SYD HEARD THE WATER running, then stop. She waited awhile longer. She didn't want him to have an excuse to escape her, because she intended to have it out right now. The fact that he'd basically be a captive in his own bathtub would only make it harder for him to think about retreating.

She made sure the kids were occupied, then headed for his room.

When Syd walked into the room, she noticed Ki's clothes flung across the bed as haphazardly made as Jamie's bed. She started to walk toward the closed bathroom door when something stopped her. That inner self-protective sense prompted her to turn around, but all she saw was his laptop computer.

She wasn't sure what made her go over to it. Maybe it was remembering the time the phone rang and something clicked in his computer. He never mentioned receiving information for an upcoming book that way before. And his attitude toward her hadn't changed until that day.

Syd never felt uneasy going through someone else's personal belongings or records. It had been part of her job for too long. But this was different. This was Ki's.

She took a deep breath and blanked her mind as she switched on the computer. The low hum sounded loud in her ears as she acquainted herself with the software and brought up the menu. Most of the files were pretty self-explanatory, dealing with his book on Thomas Baskin. A few looked to be personal and a few weren't as concise. She made her way through each one. One was letters to his agent, his mother and someone named Fran who she gathered knew Ki a lot better than Syd would like her to. Her heart stopped when she brought up the last file and began reading. She scrolled through most of it, not bothering to read. She didn't have to. She already knew what most of it said.

And the private file the agency kept on her wasn't as surprising as it might have been a year ago.

She felt a tiny rip deep within her. Was it Ki, the writer, who studied these files about her? Or Ki, her lover?

"Find anything interesting?"

She slowly turned around, keeping her hands behind her back. That way they wouldn't find their way around his neck. Even seeing him with steam floating out from the bathroom behind him, his skin still damp from his bath and a towel draped around his hips didn't change her mind.

"I had no idea the agency knew about my switching toothpaste brands," she said with an evenness that surprised her. Right now, she wanted to scream at him. To rant and rave and demand to know why he had done this to her. "And here I thought I had a few secrets. But I guess I shouldn't expect that in my business."

What she noticed most was his lack of embarrassment at being caught.

She took a deep breath.

"How did you get them?"

"Trade secret."

Syd held up her hand as if to ward him off. "What does it matter now? Do you realize what you've done? You've let them know where I am."

Ki laughed at what he considered her paranoia. "There's no way they could know. My source is very adept at getting in and out of computers. He doesn't leave any tracks."

By now Syd was furious. She was furious at Ki for doing this to her. And furious with herself for falling in love with him. "You fool! Do you honestly think ISA doesn't have traps laid out? The minute a file is pulled, there's a red flag! They'd immediately trace it to your source and there was probably a tap put on his phone before the hour was out. And he faxed it to you here." She sliced her hand through the air. "They know where I am!"

"Fine, if they know where you are, why haven't they shown up yet to drag you back to D.C.?" he demanded. "Maybe that's what you're hoping for? That they'll make your decision for you. Tell you to get your pretty little ass back to hobnobbing with those arms dealers and whatever else you used to do with them."

Syd was across the room before Ki finished his last sentence, and her hand lashed across his face so hard his head whipped to one side.

"You bastard," she hissed. "You don't know anything about what I used to do. What you read in those reports are only words. They don't detail a fraction of how I felt whenever I finished." She went over to the computer, deleted the file and switched the computer off. "You couldn't just ask me, could you?" The pain she felt was so great she couldn't hide it.

He wished he had a plausible excuse for her. "I made a mistake by asking for your file. I planned to delete it, myself, tonight. After I thought about it, I realized I should have waited for you to tell me what you wanted to tell me instead of finding out for myself."

She shook her head, denying him a chance to say anything more. She walked toward the door but stopped and turned around before opening it.

"We'll be leaving tomorrow."

"To run and hide from your Mean Mr. Leo again?" he jeered, stung by her abrupt announcement. Although, he acknowledged, it shouldn't surprise him. "Just as you've been doing? You know, you might not get so lucky with the next guy whose house you break into."

The blaze from Syd's eyes should have burst him into flames.

"How could I ever think I could love you?" She twisted the knob and walked out. The door swung shut behind her.

It wasn't until then Ki allowed his knees to give out on him. He knew to the second when Syd told the children they were leaving. The cries of dismay told him. But it was the memory of the hurt shining in Syd's eyes as she looked at him that haunted him the most. And the knowledge he'd put it there.

SYD HATED TO CRY because crying made her eyes red and swollen and caused her nose to run. In short, she was a pitiful sight. She wanted to hate Ki for making her cry, but it was hard to hate someone you loved.

"Auntie Syd." Heidi's low voice stopped her tears effectively.

She swiped her hand across her nose and turned over in bed. "What's wrong, sweetheart?"

Her lower lip trembled. "I had a bad dream. I don't want to leave here. What if Santa can't find me?"

Syd gathered her into the bed. "I thought you wanted to go back home. Besides, remember what Jamie and I told you? Santa can always find you."

"I don't want to go without Ki."

Syd blinked rapidly to keep the tears from falling. "I know, honey, but we have to."

"But I thought we were going to have Christmas here."

She only prayed she wouldn't cry now. The last thing she wanted to do was upset Heidi more. "Things changed. We're going back now."

Heidi snuggled close to her aunt. "It won't be the same without Ki," she mumbled as she fell asleep.

Syd lay awake, crying silently until sheer exhaustion took its toll.

"WHAT IF I SAID I was sorry?"

Syd had gotten up at dawn, finished the packing and had just loaded the last item into the back of her Jeep while the kids put on their coats. She turned to look at Ki, who stood nearby with Cocoa and Bogie dancing around his legs in their own bid for attention. She figured she must have looked as bad as he did.

His eyes were darkly shadowed from little sleep and his features drawn. He hadn't shaved that morning and even his hair hadn't been combed. He stood before her with a stark expression written on his face.

"Trust is very important to me, Ki," she said huskily. "I needed it in order to survive. I doubt I would have told you all that was in the file, but I would have told you enough so you would know the person I was.

Still, maybe what you did was a good thing. You know what kind of person I was and I know what kind of person you are."

He winced as her verbal dart struck home.

"Maybe it's for the best." She forced the words past a clogged throat. "Your work requires a lot of traveling, and with Jamie in school and Heidi in preschool and entering kindergarten next fall, that isn't possible. So I'm going back to Virginia, and I'm going to march into Leo's office and tell him to get off my back or else."

"Then fly back to Virginia, do that and come back here." He was past caring that he was begging. He picked up Bogie and scratched him behind his ears as he looked at Syd. "I don't want to lose you, Syd. I love you."

She refused to cry in front of him. Her chin wobbled dangerously, but she wasn't going to cry.

"I wish you had said that a little while before. Maybe it would have changed things, although I don't think it would have." She turned to see Heidi and Jamie walking slowly outside. "Come on, I want to get going."

"I don't want to go!" Heidi wailed, running toward Ki and throwing her arms around him. "You need us, Ki!"

He put Bogie down and dropped to his knees to hold her tightly against him. "Hey, don't worry, okay? Everything will be fine. You'll see," he assured her, using a corner of his shirttail to dry her tears. He urged her toward the Jeep.

Jamie stopped in front of Ki and held out his hand.

"She doesn't stay mad long," he muttered.

As if deciding a hug wouldn't be too childish, Jamie threw his arms around Ki. He bent his head and whispered something in Ki's ear.

"Be good and take care of them, Jamie," Ki said huskily when Jamie stepped back. The boy ran to the Jeep and climbed in.

That left Syd. Ki straightened up and walked toward her.

"You know, we all make mistakes," he said slowly. "I can't do anything more than apologize, and I hope one day you'll come to realize that I'd like to be in your life and I want you in mine." He tucked a small card in her jacket pocket. "It has my agent's phone number and my cellular phone number. If you ever need anything, I want you to call me."

"Our lives are moving in different directions, Ki. You're happiest on your own traveling around the country and writing your books. And I want to make a home for the kids and myself." Her voice was raw from all her crying. "I'm no longer angry at you, but I still feel it's better that we part now, rather than later when it will be harder on us and on the kids."

She reached up and pressed a light kiss against his mouth. It wasn't until she drew back that he realized his lips were salty from her tears.

"Goodbye, Ki," she murmured, hurrying back to the Jeep. She whistled for the dogs and put them in the back seat before climbing into the driver's seat.

As the truck grew smaller in the distance, Ki felt as if he was watching a part of him drive off. He slowly walked back inside the cabin. The smell of pine was everywhere. He looked at the tree with its colorful ornaments and thought how lonely it looked now.

He walked closer when he realized there were two brightly wrapped packages underneath. One much larger than the other.

For Ki from Heidi and Jamie read the label on the smaller package.

Not wanting to wait, he tore open the paper and laughed when he found a set of earplugs inside the box. And almost cried.

"You might find this will come in handy in the hot tub. Love, Syd" was written on the larger package.

Ki ripped the paper off and pulled a high-powered water gun out of the box.

He stared at two of the most incongruous gifts a man could receive. Ki knew he would never receive two gifts that would mean more to him.

"No, Leo. How many times do I have to say it?" Syd strode to the front door and pulled it open.

"You came back from California the same day I flew out there. That has to mean you miss the agency," her boss argued as he poked a cigar in his mouth.

Syd waved her hand in front of her face when it looked as if he was going to light up.

"Not in the house," she said firmly, pulling the door open. "And no, I don't miss it. I've gotten a catalog from Georgetown. I think I'll go back to get my law degree."

"Lord save us from more lawyers!" He walked outside with Syd following. She wanted to make sure he was definitely leaving. He turned around. "You were one of my best, kid. I don't know how I'm going to replace you," he said mournfully.

She resisted the urge to feel sorry for him. "I have faith in you." She kissed his cheek.

He looked around at the neatly landscaped colonial-style house and shook his head. "This isn't you, sweetheart."

"Heidi and Jamie are familiar with it. That's fine for now." Syd walked him to his car where his driver waited patiently.

Leo looked at her with the idea of trying one more time. When he read the resolve in her face he knew it was useless.

"You have a good Christmas," he said gruffly.

"Do yourself a favor, Leo, and go home and celebrate Christmas Eve with your wife," she advised. "You just might like it."

Syd remained outside, watching Leo's car drive off. She was still tired from her marathon drive back to Virginia. But she wanted them to be back before Christmas. She'd found and decorated a tree, although not with half the enthusiasm she'd put into the tree in Tahoe. She resolutely tried to put Ki out of her mind, but she found it wasn't all that easy.

Every night, she lay in bed wishing he was lying beside her. Even the dogs searched the house for a fourth person.

Syd had used the drive back to mull over the days spent with Ki and what he had done. She still felt his getting hold of her records was wrong, but she knew she was wrong in running away. He was right. She had been running from Leo because she didn't want to confront the issue. And she had run from Ki because it was easier than confronting him. She'd had enough confrontation in dealing with Shane's and Jenny's deaths. She wondered if he would talk to her if she called him after the holidays.

She started back for the house with the intention of letting the dogs back in. Bogie had taken an immediate dislike to Leo and was put outside before he took a chunk out of Leo's leg.

She had just turned around when the sound of a car alerted her to company.

"It's too early for the kids to be back," she murmured. A neighbor had asked if they could come over for a Christmas Eve childrens' party that afternoon, and Syd had said yes since she thought it would be good for them. She remained on the front step, watching a dark sedan make its way up the curving driveway. She couldn't quite make out the driver, but there was something about him...

She grew very still as she watched the car roll to a stop and the driver climb out.

"Damn cars have no guts," Ki grumbled. He looked up and caught Syd's eyes on him. The naked longing he felt was reflected in her gaze. "Jamie told me your address."

She licked her lips as she tried to form the right words.

"Why did you come?"

"A car passed me with a man sitting in the back seat who looked as if he'd shoot his best friend on a bet, and he was chewing on a cigar. Sound like anyone you know?'' He couldn't stop looking at her. She looked beautiful even dressed in leg-hugging jeans and a salmon-colored sweater that hung loosely around her hips.

She stared at him as if afraid he'd disappear if she looked away. "Leo wanted to try one more time."

He remained by the car door. After all, he might be out of here in the next ten seconds. "What did you tell him?"

"I told him what I've always told him. Except this time he believed me." She felt as if the few feet between them was a hundred. "I told him I picked up a catalog at Georgetown. I'm thinking of going back to law school."

Ki grew very still. "There are good law schools in California."

"But I don't live in California." She stepped carefully. She was still hurting. She didn't want to hurt anymore.

"I have a house there, although I don't use it very much. I only bought it for a tax write-off," he explained. "Or, if you think it would be better for the kids, we could live here."

Syd was so afraid to hope for the best. "What about your books?"

"I'd have to do some traveling for them, but not as much as I do now," he explained. "And there's no reason why I can't just gather up my information and go home to write the book. Besides, you pick out some points I don't always notice." He closed the door and walked slowly toward her. "When we were young and stupid, my three buddies and I took a vow we'd never get married. If all goes well, Deke's going to win the title of World's Last Bachelor. Funny thing is, that's one title I don't mind losing—if you're willing to marry me.''

Syd's body jerked. "Marry?" she uttered the word as if unable to believe it.

He nodded as he stopped in front of her. "What better combination can you think of than a true-crime writer and an ex-spy turned lawyer?" His green eyes softened. "Ah, Syd, I love you so much it hurts. When you left the cabin, I felt like sitting down and bawling like a baby. And then I found my gifts."

"Did you open them?" she asked in a small voice, already seeing her answer in his eyes that shimmered, just as her own eyes filled with tears.

"Yeah, and then I did bawl." A crooked smile curved his mouth. "Will you marry me, Sydney Ann Taylor? I think I'd like to be around when Heidi gets to dating age and you handle her overeager boy-friends. Those guys will never know what hit them."

"Oh, Ki." Her voice was hushed and for once she didn't tamp down her emotions. Syd threw herself into Ki's arms and returned his kiss as hotly and eagerly as he offered it. "I've missed you so much. I was so stupid not to talk it out with you. I wish I had. I'm not going to run anymore," she murmured, digging into his waistband and pulling his shirt out. She had the sudden desperate need to feel his skin.

"Honey, as much as I like what you're doing, we're out here in the open," he mumbled even as his hands found their way under her sweater. He swore under his breath when he discovered she wasn't wearing a bra.

"And I'd hate to give the kids an early sex education."

"They're at a party," she told him in a breathless voice.

Ki picked her up and carried her into the house as she offered directions to her bedroom.

"So, does this mean you're going to marry me?" he asked as he slammed the front door closed after them.

Epilogue

Nine months later

"You worm! You dirty rat! You slime!"

Ki looked up from his trusty laptop computer set on the table in front of him. In deference to the hot summer afternoon, he'd sat outside to work on his latest book—a woman who had held her husband a sex slave for three years, then killed him.

"Is something wrong?" he asked mildly as his obviously furious wife advanced on him.

"You know very well something is wrong! Did you think I wouldn't hear you on the phone to Deke?" Syd rolled up a magazine and hit him in the stomach with it. He winced under her attack. "You gave him our tickets to Paris!"

Ki winced. "It was for a good reason," he explained. "Besides, I didn't think it would be a good idea for you to travel in your condition."

"I'm pregnant, you nitwit, not dead!" she shrieked, picking up another magazine and throwing it at him. "You promised me those days in Paris. We decided once the kids were settled in school and we knew the live-in housekeeper would work out, we would go.'' She advanced on him looking like a pregnant whirlwind.

With her narrow frame, she also looked as if she had swallowed a basketball. Ki sometimes wondered if she would have any trouble in delivering. He didn't believe the doctor's assurances that nature takes that into account.

"Syd, you already look eight months' pregnant even though you're not that close," he reminded her. As if either of them could forget the particular night she conceived! He was glad both Heidi and Jamie were looking forward to the arrival of their new cousin. "I don't want you to deliver during the flight." Sweat popped out in tiny beads across his forehead as he thought of her going into labor where they wouldn't have any medical assistance. It was the nightmare of every airplane disaster movie made.

"We're taking the Concorde, you nitwit. There wouldn't be enough time." She started to lower herself into the chair next to his, but Ki's arms snaked out and pulled her onto his lap.

"I'm too heavy." She sniffed.

Ki smiled. He was getting used to her mood swings. True to her nature, Syd never believed in doing things in halfway measures.

"We'll go as soon as the baby is old enough," he assured her, folding her as close to him as her large stomach would allow. "I promise."

She eventually got her trembling lower lip under control. "You could get two more tickets," she ventured.

Ki kissed the corner of her mouth. "Syd, I plan to be in the delivery room with you. Don't make it be the aisle of a jet."

"I don't know why. You'll probably pass out once things get hairy," she muttered, fingering his shirt button and releasing it from the buttonhole. She idly drew patterns on his chest. "The kids won't be back for a couple more hours," she murmured, nuzzling his neck. She grazed the skin with her teeth and growled under her breath.

"I had no idea pregnant women could be so sexy. Or so horny," he teased. "And you might as well quit the seduction tactics. I still intend to be with you every step of the way when you go into labor."

Syd's eyes gleamed with fervor. "A bet. If you don't pass out in the delivery room, once the doctor gives his okay, I will give you an erotic weekend the likes of which you'll never forget."

He felt as if he was walking into a trap. "And if I do?" Which he couldn't imagine happening. Not after the years he had spent viewing police photographs.

"You take me to Paris."

"I'll already be doing that."

"Not *my* idea of Paris." She leaned back so she could see his face better. "Well?"

"Deal."

Syd covered Ki's mouth with a kiss to seal their pact.

"You'll love my Paris," she murmured.

"Just get plenty of rest for my weekend," he suggested, gently rubbing her belly and chuckling when the baby kicked out against his hand. "Good thing we aren't going. This kid wants out real fast. Are you sure we're not having twins?"

"I told you what the doctor told me. The ultrasound showed only one, but sometimes one baby hides the second and one heartbeat can be masked by the other." She winced at another energetic kick inside her abdomen. "Right now, I wouldn't be surprised if there were triplets in there."

TRUE TO KI'S PREDICTION, Syd delivered twin boys the day they would have left on the Concorde.

True to Syd's prediction, Ki got only so far during the delivery procedure before he made the mistake of looking at the instruments and passed out cold.

Syd gave Ki his adults-only weekend, anyway, since she knew she would enjoy their time together just as much as he would.

It was no surprise when she gave birth to twin girls nine months after their time in Paris.

Syd didn't miss the danger and Ki didn't miss the travel. They had too much adventure going on in their own home.

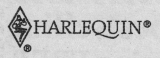 **HARLEQUIN®**

The proprietors of Weddings, Inc. hope you have enjoyed visiting Eternity, Massachusetts. And if you missed any of the exciting Weddings, Inc. titles, here is your opportunity to complete your collection:

Harlequin Superromance	#598	*Wedding Invitation* by Marisa Carroll	$3.50 U.S. ☐ $3.99 CAN. ☐
Harlequin Romance	#3319	*Expectations* by Shannon Waverly	$2.99 U.S. ☐ $3.50 CAN. ☐
Harlequin Temptation	#502	*Wedding Song* by Vicki Lewis Thompson	$2.99 U.S. ☐ $3.50 CAN. ☐
Harlequin American Romance	#549	*The Wedding Gamble* by Muriel Jensen	$3.50 U.S. ☐ $3.99 CAN. ☐
Harlequin Presents	#1692	*The Vengeful Groom* by Sara Wood	$2.99 U.S. ☐ $3.50 CAN. ☐
Harlequin Intrigue	#298	*Edge of Eternity* by Jasmine Cresswell	$2.99 U.S. ☐ $3.50 CAN. ☐
Harlequin Historical	#248	*Vows* by Margaret Moore	$3.99 U.S. ☐ $4.50 CAN. ☐

HARLEQUIN BOOKS...
NOT THE SAME OLD STORY

TOTAL AMOUNT	$
POSTAGE & HANDLING	$
($1.00 for one book, 50¢ for each additional)	
APPLICABLE TAXES*	$ _____
TOTAL PAYABLE	$ _____
(check or money order—please do not send cash)	

To order, complete this form and send it, along with a check or money order for the total above, payable to Harlequin Books, to: **In the U.S.:** 3010 Walden Avenue, P.O. Box 9047, Buffalo, NY 14269-9047; **In Canada:** P.O. Box 613, Fort Erie, Ontario, L2A 5X3.

Name: _____

Address: _____ City: _____

State/Prov.: _____ Zip/Postal Code: _____

*New York residents remit applicable sales taxes.
 Canadian residents remit applicable GST and provincial taxes.

WED-F

Take 4 bestselling love stories FREE

Plus get a FREE surprise gift!

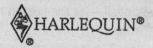

CHRISTMAS STALKINGS

All wrapped up in spine-tingling packages, here are three books guaranteed to chill your spine...and warm your hearts this holiday season!

#302 THE KID WHO STOLE CHRISTMAS
Linda Stevens

#303 I'LL BE HOME FOR CHRISTMAS
Dawn Stewardson

#304 BEARING GIFTS
Aimée Thurlo

This December, fill your stockings with the "Christmas Stalkings"—for the best in romantic suspense. Only from

HARLEQUIN®

INTRIGUE®

HIXM

HARLEQUIN® AMERICAN ROMANCE®

Four sexy hunks who vowed they'd never take "the vow" of marriage...

What happens to this Bachelor Club when, one by one, they find the right bachelorette?

Meet four of the most perfect men:

Steve: **THE MARRYING TYPE**
Judith Arnold
(October)

Tripp: **ONCE UPON A HONEYMOON**
Julie Kistler
(November)

Ukiah: **HE'S A REBEL**
Linda Randall Wisdom
(December)

Deke: **THE WORLD'S LAST BACHELOR**
Pamela Browning
(January)

STUDSG-R

On the most romantic day of the year, capture the thrill of falling in love all over again—with

Harlequin's

Bachelors

They're three sexy and *very single* men who run very special personal ads to find the women of their fantasies by Valentine's Day. These exciting, passion-filled stories are written by bestselling Harlequin authors.

Your Heart's Desire by Elise Title
Mr. Romance by Pamela Bauer
Sleepless in St. Louis by Tiffany White

Be sure not to miss Harlequin's Valentine Bachelors, available in February wherever Harlequin books are sold.

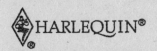
HARLEQUIN®

VB

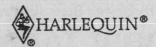
HARLEQUIN®

Don't miss these Harlequin favorites by some of our most distinguished authors!
And now you can receive a discount by ordering two or more titles!

HT#25483	BABYCAKES by Glenda Sanders	$2.99	☐
HT#25559	JUST ANOTHER PRETTY FACE by Candace Schuler	$2.99	☐
HP#11608	SUMMER STORMS by Emma Goldrick	$2.99	☐
HP#11632	THE SHINING OF LOVE by Emma Darcy	$2.99	☐
HR#03265	HERO ON THE LOOSE by Rebecca Winters	$2.89	☐
HR#03268	THE BAD PENNY by Susan Fox	$2.99	☐
HS#70532	TOUCH THE DAWN by Karen Young	$3.39	☐
HS#70576	ANGELS IN THE LIGHT by Margot Dalton	$3.50	☐
HI#22249	MUSIC OF THE MIST by Laura Pender	$2.99	☐
HI#22267	CUTTING EDGE by Caroline Burnes	$2.99	☐
HAR#16489	DADDY'S LITTLE DIVIDEND by Elda Minger	$3.50	☐
HAR#16525	CINDERMAN by Anne Stuart	$3.50	☐
HH#28801	PROVIDENCE by Miranda Jarrett	$3.99	☐
HH#28775	A WARRIOR'S QUEST by Margaret Moore	$3.99	☐

(limited quantities available on certain titles)

TOTAL AMOUNT	$
DEDUCT: 10% DISCOUNT FOR 2+ BOOKS	$
POSTAGE & HANDLING	$
($1.00 for one book, 50¢ for each additional)	
APPLICABLE TAXES*	$_____
TOTAL PAYABLE	$_____

(check or money order—please do not send cash)

To order, complete this form and send it, along with a check or money order for the total above, payable to Harlequin Books, to: **In the U.S.:** 3010 Walden Avenue, P.O. Box 9047, Buffalo, NY 14269-9047; **In Canada:** P.O. Box 613, Fort Erie, Ontario, L2A 5X3.

Name: _____

Address: _____City: _____

State/Prov.: _____ Zip/Postal Code: _____

*New York residents remit applicable sales taxes.
 Canadian residents remit applicable GST and provincial taxes.

HBACK-OD